"You always have my attention."

He always would. When she left this time, a part of her would remain behind. She'd also carry with her the longing to touch him. To be with him. She'd learned something else by being home these two weeks: she didn't relax. She was constantly moving or doing something. If she kept moving, the silence didn't creep in.

She sipped her water. "You asked me what I do for fun. The answer is I don't know what to do when I stop traveling."

He reached for her hand. "You sit in Labelle's with me and drink a milkshake. We can hang out anytime."

He made the answer seem so simple and how she wished it was. The waitress approached and set down Luke's soda and Shelby's chocolate shake. The dairy served its shakes and sodas in clear, double-walled, rippled goblets. Shelby picked up the long-handled spoon and lifted out the cherry. She held it out to Luke. When he took the stem out of his mouth, he'd tied it into a bow.

"Still don't know how you do that." Shelby stirred the whipped cream into her shake.

"My one special but odd talent that serves absolutely no purpose but to make a great party trick." He set the twisted stem on the tabletop. "So do you fear anything?"

Losing you.

Dear Reader,

Shelby and Luke's story came to life after I crewed a hot-air balloon race. At the postrace banquet, my friends said, "You should write a book where the owners of an inn also fly a hot-air balloon," and intrigued, I did just that and you hold the results in your hand.

Shelby Bien never comes home for more than a few days at a time. As a globe-trotting photographer, she's all about her career, even if that means hanging off cliffs to get the perfect shot. Besides, the small historic town of her childhood reminds her of getting her heart broken by Luke Thornburg, her first love and boy next door. But Luke needs Shelby's help. Their fathers' feud means the town's balloon won't fly in the town's annual race unless Shelby pilots. Together, she and Luke can salvage the town's pride. Trouble is, soaring over the landscape means all sorts of feelings return, and Shelby can't risk her heart again.

I hope you enjoy this second-chance-at-love story. It's my debut for Harlequin Special Edition, and I'm excited to be writing for the line. Stay tuned for the rest of the Love in the Valley series, and sign up for my newsletter at micheledunaway.com.

All the best,

Michele

What Happens in the Air

MICHELE DUNAWAY

HARLEQUIN

SPECIAL
EDITION

ISBN-13: 978-1-335-72448-9

What Happens in the Air

Copyright © 2023 by Michele Dunaway

Harlequin Enterprises ULC
22 Adelaide St. West, 41st Floor
Toronto, Ontario M5H 4E3, Canada
www.Harlequin.com

Printed in U.S.A.

In first grade, **Michele Dunaway** knew she wanted to be a teacher when she grew up. By second grade, she wanted to be an author. By third grade, she decided to be both. Born and raised in Missouri, Michele lives in her childhood hometown and travels frequently, with the places she visits inspiring her writing. A teacher by day and novelist by night, Michele describes herself as a woman who does too much but doesn't know how to stop, especially when it comes to baking brownies and chocolate chip cookies.

Books by Michele Dunaway

Harlequin Special Edition

Love in the Valley

What Happens in the Air

Visit the Author Profile page
at Harlequin.com for more titles.

First and foremost, I dedicate this to my agent, Jennifer Herrington, for believing. You know without me saying exactly how much this means. Here's to many, many more. Next to my high school classmate Kim Loomis for inviting me to my first balloon race and to Keith and Michelle Lutz who let me crew and answered dozens of questions. To Kasey Michaels for honesty in editing, Jodi Thomas for working your magic and to my fabulous critique partners Susan Alyworth, Sharon Hartley and Patricia Forsythe for words of wisdom. To my editor, Megan Broderick, for loving this book, to my LRW friends and to my readers who let me come into your lives and tell stories. This one is for you.

Prologue

Ten, nine, eight... As the crowd in Times Square counted down, Shelby's gaze shifted from the TV screen in the third-floor living room to the figure who'd appeared in the doorway. Her heart jumped. He'd made it.

"Sorry, I'm late. You know how Aunt Edna is," Luke Thornburg said. He reached for her hand, helping her out of her favorite overstuffed chair. Little tingles ran up her arm. "Come on."

Hand in hand, they raced down the wide center hallway to the balcony overlooking Main Street. Luke threw open the door and they stepped into the brisk winter air. Down below, revelers on the streets of Beaumont cheered as the clock hit zero.

The fireworks would start when the church bells

stopped chiming, and Luke lifted Shelby's chin and lowered his mouth to hers. She savored the softness of his lips and the touch of his tongue. He drew back and swiped his finger over her cheek. "Happy New Year, Shelby."

She would not cry. She'd be brave. "Happy New Year, Luke."

He kissed her again, and as the last chime faded away, he dropped an arm over her shoulders and turned them so they faced the riverfront. "Look!"

The first fireworks whizzed into the sky and, seconds later, burst into a cascade of red stars. She settled into his arms. For most of her seventeen years, she and Luke had watched the celebratory Missouri River fireworks show from this exact spot. They'd known one another forever, after all. But tonight was the first time they'd watched as a couple. They'd started dating in September, right before homecoming. Over winter break, they'd taken the next step, making love. Tonight was their last night together until he returned in June from a semester abroad. She'd miss him terribly.

Luke drew her even closer. "Aunt Edna kept talking. I couldn't get away."

"It's okay." She'd met Aunt Edna and understood. Still, during the wait, Shelby had nibbled off her lip gloss. A self-described tomboy, she'd worn the faint pink color because dressing up for New Year's Eve was family tradition and she'd wanted Luke to remember her as fancy and pretty. She wrapped her arms around his waist. Despite herself, she was nervous. She never should have listened to Maren—their new friend who'd moved to Beaumont right before Thanksgiving. Maren maintained Luke was after one thing—sex—and once Shelby put out, he'd be like most guys and dump her. After all, Maren said, who could fault him if he wanted freedom from entanglements while in London?

Secure in his arms, Shelby shoved away any lingering doubts. Luke was only a few months older and her best friend. Their fathers had served in the military together, so their parents had been friends forever and next-door neighbors almost as long. Shelby's childhood pictures had Luke and/or his parents in them. They'd shared milestones: from first steps, to learning to fish, to crewing their families' hot-air balloon, to being each other's first kiss, and then first lovers. More fireworks burst over the sky.

"I can tell you're sad, you know," Luke said. "June will be here before we know it."

She couldn't be selfish. The semester abroad was such a great opportunity for him. "Nine a.m. flight, right?"

"Yeah. I'm nervous," he admitted.

"You'll do great," she encouraged, trying to remain upbeat.

His tone turned wistful. "Except I'm going to miss

taking you to prom. Email me pictures of your dress. And email me every day. And keep taking pictures."

Shelby forced a smile, for whenever she thought of his leaving, her heart hurt. But she'd encouraged him to go. Luke had finished all his high school credits a semester early, and it was a great opportunity for him to attend this educational program in England. She herself would travel the world if given the chance. "You know it. And I'm excited to try out my new camera."

Her parents had given her a DSLR camera for Christmas, and Luke had accompanied her when she'd tested it out. Eventually she hoped to see all the places she read about in the *Global Outdoors* magazine her parents bought for the inn's guest parlor. "Dad said we've got a world-famous photographer staying with us in a few weeks. Maybe she'll give me some pointers."

Cheers erupted from the people below on Main Street as more vivid shades of red, green, yellow and blue boomed overhead.

Luke pushed back his dark blond hair. "My leaving won't change anything," he promised as orange flames bloomed across the clear night. Somewhere along the line he'd grown half a head taller. His cheekbones had become more defined and chiseled. He smelled divine——like a spice with a hint of sage.

But leaving would change things, Shelby knew. Besides missing prom, he wouldn't see her make her first flight as a hot-air-balloon pilot, a goal she'd been working toward for almost two years. Curling her fingers into his jacket, she gripped tight as glittery silver fireworks zigzagged and swooshed. Her breath made small clouds in the chilly air. Jittery nerves made her poke him directly below his left rib. His childhood body had been replaced by rock-solid muscle—her family and his had celebrated his eighteenth birthday the day after Thanksgiving.

"Hey, stop that. I'm bigger, you know."

She clung to their easy teasing. "I'm not scared of you."

"You should be. I'm older and wiser."

"By two whole months." He laughed with the deep throaty sound she liked and a mouth that made her tingle all over whenever he kissed her. Which he now did.

"Still older," he said as he broke the kiss. "I'll miss that when I'm gone." His gaze sharpened. "I'll miss *you*."

More fireworks shot forth and began booming, but rather than watching them, Shelby focused on how the bright lights reflected like flames in Luke's brown eyes. The colors highlighted a jawline covered with light stubble. "When I said I loved you, I meant it."

"I know. I love you, too." Without letting go, she faced the river. When she and Luke had been younger, they'd stood here and searched for river pirates. They'd pretended to be riverboat captains, or explorers surveying uncharted land. When they'd entered their teens, they'd discussed homework assignments, or later, their first crushes. None of her or Luke's crushes had ever rated a second date.

Luke made her laugh. He kept her secrets. He held her when she cried. Once he'd carried her home half a mile after she'd sprained her ankle. The tingly warmth of his body kept the chill at bay. He was her other half.

No other boy held a candle to him. And when they'd sealed their love? The three waterfall fireworks that overlapped in a loud, colorful symphony in the finale couldn't begin to compare to the sparks of their lovemaking. Below, the revelers oohed and aahed but, for Shelby, impending loss settled like a rock in her stomach. The middle of June was a lifetime away.

Down below, partygoers returned inside. Luke and Shelby remained at the railing, watching the plumes of residual gray smoke dissipate. Heading into the brightness meant saying goodbye. A horn blared below and they instinctively turned toward each other. Luke leaned his forehead against hers. Warm hands slid up to cup her cheeks. "You're freezing."

"I'm fine," she lied. Her flats, cream tights and plaid dress, so perfect for the inn's annual Ring-in-the-New-Year party inside, didn't keep away the chill like the heavy sweater, jeans and boots he was wearing.

"Your teeth are chattering." But instead of moving toward the door, his thumbs slid to her mouth— right thumb pressed to her bottom lip—and Shelby sucked in an anticipatory breath.

"We're going to be okay, Shelby."

While time could do nothing but march forward, for a brief moment, the world slowed. Paused, as Luke brought his lips softly to hers like a butterfly's landing. "I love you."

The kiss deepened and sent Shelby spiraling until they heard her dad as he shouted, "Are you two up there?"

Shelby's eyelids snapped open. Luke dropped his hands. Fumbling for composure, she stepped into the bright hallway. "Yep. Fireworks just finished."

Shelby's dad gaze flickered between the two of them, his face unreadable as he took in her swollen lips. "Time to call it a night." To Luke, he said, "Your parents and Aunt Edna walked home already."

"Thanks. Happy New Year, Shelby." Luke took the back stairs two at a time.

"Everything okay?" her dad asked.

She would not cry at the interrupted goodbye. Once they'd told their parents they were dating, both of their dads had started checking on them. Her mom had even given her the sex talk—an awkward experience.

"I'll miss him. He's my best friend." Voicing facts didn't lessen the hurt.

Her dad's big-bear hugs normally made things better, but not this time. "I know it's hard. But he'll be back in June. Until then, you'll have prom and graduation and… My princess going off to college in August? Say it isn't so."

She wiggled to get free. "Dad."

He released her with a last ruffle of her pixie cut. She entered her bedroom, closed the door and flopped down on the huge four-poster with a pink floral bedspread.

A light soon flashed from the window of the three-story building next door. Shelby grabbed the flashlight she kept on a bedside table and plunged her room into darkness. In middle school, she and Luke had learned Morse code in Explorers. They'd become so proficient they'd won a competition, and with a limited cell-phone calling plan and no data, sending messages became their thing.

"We'll see each other when I get back," Luke sent. "First thing."

"Okay," Shelby returned.

"I love you."

"Me, too."

"I'm going to miss you."

"Me, too."

"Write me."

"I will. Every day."

"Do not forget."

"I won't," she promised, meaning every long and short pulse of light she used to create the words.

"Pinkie swear." He used the term from when they'd been seven and determined that swearing loyalty was the best way to keep each other's secrets. So far they'd never betrayed that trust.

Missing him already, a tear threatened as she signaled back, "I love you. Forever friends. Pinkie swear."

Fate would make a liar of them both.

Chapter One

Twelve years later

Sometimes you got lucky. You were in the right place at the exact right time. When the road forked, it led somewhere great.

Or you at least found somewhere you could lose yourself, Shelby decided. If only for a little while.

Today was one of those times. Shelby turned off US 61, exiting the most direct route from eastern Iowa City to Beaumont, Missouri. Watching the road, sky and GPS, she made a few sharp turns before wedging her hybrid into a safe parking spot along the gravel shoulder. Flashers on, she killed the engine and reached into the black nylon bag sitting on the passenger seat. She took out her favorite DSLR, stepped out into the September air and swung the lens upward.

Pure impulse had struck two miles back when she'd first seen the red-and-white hot-air balloon. The candy-cane-striped balloon's lower altitude indicated the pilot was searching for a safe landing spot, and as Shelby had been in the car for about three hours, she needed to stretch her legs, anyway. She'd changed course and given chase.

Besides, every photographer had a story about stumbling on fantastic, spur-of-the-moment shots, and how long had it been since she'd photographed a subject simply for no other reason than pure joy? Photographing hot-air balloons also reminded her of her childhood, and that's where she was headed. Home.

Currently ahead of schedule on a cross-country photography assignment for *Global Outdoors* magazine, she had the time to veer off course and take some spur of the moment photos before she reached her parents' inn. While she wouldn't be able to visit with her parents long, whenever she was in this part of the country Shelby made sure to stop by. She'd surprise them later today by arriving a day earlier than expected.

Shelby shimmied over the rattling, black metal tube gate, then landed, hiking boots first, in a recently mowed pasture containing grazing black Angus cattle. Their meal interrupted by the whooshing sound of the pilot firing the burners and venting the crown, the animals trotted off as the balloon descended. The wicker

basket bounced once but didn't tip upon touchdown—
how many times had she tumbled out when the envelope began to drag? She grinned. Far too many to
count. Four passengers laughed and clapped as their
ride came to an end.

Shelby kept her finger on the shutter release, the
camera constantly clicking as she captured the moment.
She photographed the chase vehicle as it arrived—a
huge diesel crew cab pulling a trailer. Following it was
a smaller SUV. A farmer let both through the gate.

She'd participated in the familiar scene many times:
first as an occupant riding along, then as part of the
crew laying out the lines, and then as a pilot herself,
able to fly both balloons and single-engine planes.

She began to close the gap to the basket, but hesitated as her viewfinder revealed the younger male
passenger dropping to one knee. He opened a small
velvet box and said something that made another
male passenger put his hands to his cheeks before
answering with a loud and resounding "yes!" Ring
placed on his finger, he threw his arms around his
fiancé and kissed him soundly the moment he re-
gained footing. Then the newly man engaged held
out his left hand and the diamond-studded band to
the applause of those standing around—the pilot, the
two other passengers, who looked like his parents,
the chase crew, the SUV occupants and the farmer.
Someone popped a bottle of champagne. Shelby's

photographer's instinct functioned with automatic muscle memory as she captured the scene.

She lowered her camera after someone raised a toast with plastic flutes. She'd show off an engagement ring and celebrate, too…if she ever found the right guy. Maybe, at thirty and continuously single, she should lower her impossible standards and date more. Then again, why? A permanent relationship wasn't in the cards—she was always traveling to the next exotic location, exactly like she'd once dreamed. Even this road trip across America meant she wouldn't return to her apartment in Seattle for another month, and then would only leave again after a few days. Her fake ficus collected so much dust she really should give it away.

Camera lowered, she introduced herself and exchanged information with the happy couple so she could send them copies of the photos. Behind them, the crew deflated the envelope, which was the part of the balloon filled with air, and unclipped the ropes. The pilot's head shot up when he heard her last name. "Bien? Any relation to John Bien of JBMT ballooning?"

"Yes," Shelby said warmly. "My father."

"Heard about your dad's broken arm. Shame he and Mike won't be flying in either of the two Missouri races coming up. Great guys. Helped me out of a jam once. Tell 'em Caleb Munson says hi."

"I'll be sure to tell them." As he walked away,

Shelby frowned and returned to her vehicle. Caleb's words didn't make sense. The only thing ever grounding her dad and Mike Thornburg was an uncooperative Mother Nature. As close as brothers for the past twenty years after leaving the military, the two men had experienced unparalleled success in both their businesses and hot-air-balloon racing.

She'd find out soon enough. She planned to surprise her parents by arriving a full day early, making her standard forty-eight-hour visit almost seventy-two. As the satellite radio station blared to life with the latest pop hit, Shelby's tires crunched over loose gravel as she navigated back to the main highway.

Several hours later, nostalgia hit the moment her car began vibrating over the centuries-old bricks of Main Street that had been unearthed by the town's council twenty-three years ago. As she drove down Main, a welcome *bumpety-bump-bump* said that she was "almost there." As she passed by familiar storefronts and restaurants, the stress of the drive peeled away with every rattling jolt.

Beaumont never seemed to change—the redbrick or white quarried stone historic buildings dated back to the late 1700s, when westward explorers had used the Missouri River town as a launch point. Now each intersection allowed for a view down the cross street to the slow-moving river.

She opened the driver's window, letting in mid-September air that contained a hint of pending fall.

She'd stayed in Seattle following college, a logical choice as *Global Outdoors* could quickly send her abroad from Sea-Tac airport to anywhere, from Asia to New York. But no matter how far and wide she'd traveled, visiting Beaumont meant returning to familiarity and roots.

Shelby inhaled a deep, humid breath, and with it, a pungent whiff of the hickory smoke from Miller's Grill—Mr. Miller made the best barbeque found anywhere, especially the brisket and pulled pork.

Another mandatory stop was Auntie Jayne's Cookies. A rare curbside spot beckoned, and Shelby parallel-parked. She climbed the small flight of stairs and a bell jangled over the royal blue painted door. The elderly woman behind the counter lifted her head and stopped reading *People* magazine. "Shelby? What a surprise!"

Shelby grinned. "It will be. My parents are expecting me tomorrow."

"They'll be delighted." Jayne James wiped her hands on her blue gingham apron. "Let me look at you. I don't think I've seen you since for what, four years? Normally my daughter Zoe's here."

Mrs. James gave Shelby a once-over and Shelby endured the scrutiny. A late bloomer, her last growth spurt had been the summer following high school, when she'd topped out at five-nine. Shelby reached up to ensure the ponytail holder remained in place. If not, her dark hair would fall to her shoulders.

"What can I get you? Chocolate-chip still your favorite?"

Shelby grinned. "You know it. I'll take three dozen assorted with extra emphasis on the chocolate chips." Shelby checked her silver explorer watch, which confirmed she'd arrived in plenty of time for the inn's afternoon tea service.

Mrs. James snagged a square of waxed paper from the pop-up box and handed Shelby a chocolate-chip cookie, which looked like a delicious sombrero because of the extra scoop of dough on top. "See if they're as good as you remember."

Shelby bit into the edge, and sweet brown-sugar flavor made her taste buds do a happy dance. Shelby waved the cookie before taking another bite. "This is delicious. Better than the finest Paris macaron."

Mrs. James brushed away the compliment and busied herself with loading cookies into a white paper box. "Snickerdoodles, your second favorite if my memory serves."

Mrs. James's memory could give an elephant a run for his money. Nothing on Main Street ever got past her. "Yes, but better give me some oatmeal raisin, sprinkle and sugar cookies so there's a nice variety," Shelby said. "Ooh, and some of those chocolate ones with the white chips."

"Will do. So have you seen Luke yet? He's moved back."

She hid her surprise and dismay by nibbling the cookie. "No. I didn't know he was in town."

Her parents hadn't said anything. Were they afraid if she found out he'd moved home she'd find some excuse to skip even the shortest visit? As she had so many times before?

Thankfully Mrs. James didn't notice Shelby's discomfort and instead was starting to fill cookie boxes. "You two were always off on some adventure. I remember how you both would run down that sidewalk after church as fast your little legs could carry you, trying to see who could reach the door first. You look as if you could beat him now."

"Uh, thanks." A daily workout regimen kept her in top shape, a requirement for the physicality of her job. It still bothered her that altitude sickness had kept her from leaving base camp and summiting Everest. She'd prepped a year for that.

"Such a terrible tragedy about Maren. To lose her like that. She was your best friend, wasn't she?"

Trying not to bristle, Shelby kept her tone even as she set the record straight. "No, she moved here in November. We hung out a few times after Luke went to London, but then I left for Wyoming."

"Oh, that's right. The contest."

"Yes." The prize for winning a national photo contest—which the photographer at the inn had told her about—had been a three-month field experience. Slightly jealous of Luke's adventures in Europe,

which he'd told her about in full detail in early correspondence, photography had helped ease the empti-
ness. He hadn't been at her locker between class. He
hadn't sat next to her at lunch and swiped her French
fries. He hadn't helped her with her AP Chemistry homework. Losing her other half had made her
feel adrift. Was that why she'd allowed Maren into
her headspace, let her sow the seeds of doubt? Then
Shelby entered and won…and when Luke returned
from Europe, Shelby had been in Cheyenne.

Maren had been waiting in Beaumont.

And all these years later there was little point in
telling Mrs. James how a lifetime of friendship and
love between Luke and Shelby had disappeared in
an instant following a huge, long-distance fight. College and internships, and then her job, had kept her
busy and far from home.

She'd been asleep in the Serengeti when Luke and
Maren had announced their engagement on Christmas Eve. At a weather station in Antarctica when
they'd married in a small ceremony in Cincinnati,
where Maren and Luke had lived following college.
The top of Machu Picchu when their daughter was
born. Deep in the depths of the Amazon when Maren
had passed from a fast-acting cancer two years ago—
Shelby hadn't even known Maren had been sick. By
the time she'd returned to civilization, her parents
had signed her name to the flowers, card and dona-

tion, and sent her the obituary notice in one of their emails.

Her parents knew her work came first. She'd already achieved milestones—she was the youngest photographer at *Global Outdoors* and its only full-time female. With other magazines fighting to survive and cutting permanent staff in favor of using freelancers, Shelby knew her job could be here today and gone tomorrow should *Global Outdoors* follow suit. Hard work, not luck, had kept her in the game.

Not that Shelby regretted winning the contest. Childhood dreams were for children and she'd grown up. Life was best lived·being in the present.

Cookie devoured, Shelby wiped her lips with a brown paper napkin and put it and the wax paper in the trashcan. A colorful flyer advertised the weekend's fall festival. "Dad told me the inn's booked."

Mrs. James loaded oatmeal raisins next. "The festival will be busy. You caught me in a rare moment of calm. Are you staying long?"

"Until Monday morning. I figured I'd take photos of *Playgroup*, too. They usually fly the weekend before the state race."

Mrs. James paused midway through filling the last box. "Then you don't know."

The unsettlement Shelby experienced in the Iowa farm field returned. "Know what? My dad won't let a broken arm keep him from a practice. Even if he misses the state race next weekend, the town one's the weekend after. Plenty of time."

Mrs. James's face wove into concerned lines. "Oh, dear. He and Mike aren't speaking, much less flying. The town sponsorship is in limbo for both weekends."

"What?" Frowning, Shelby passed over her credit card, but Mrs. James waved away the plastic with a flick of her hand.

"Consider these a welcome-home gift. Or a bribe. Maybe it's good you're here. Maybe you can talk some sense into your dad. We've all tried and failed. Do you still fly?"

She did, but… A wrinkle deepened between Shelby's eyebrows. While Mrs. James's words helped clarify what Caleb Munson meant this morning, Shelby didn't understand how two lifelong best friends weren't speaking, much less racing. Then again, look at her and Luke. "My parents didn't say anything."

Mrs. James pushed the filled boxes a few inches in Shelby's direction. "I'm sure they didn't want to worry you. Been almost two months since your dad and Mike spoke to each other. And that was yelling."

"They've worked through issues before." Surely during the course of forty years there had been some disagreements between her dad and Luke's father, right?

"Not this time. You know the run-down bar on North Main?"

"Yeah." Attracting mostly college kids, Caldwell's could get rowdy depending on the band playing. However, it was an institution.

"Last January the new city-council members took office, including your dad."

Shelby knew this. She'd celebrated her dad's November win via video call, as she'd been in Singapore.

Mrs. James didn't miss a beat. "Mike bought Caldwell's in February. In March, the council decided North Main should be family friendly and passed an ordinance requiring liquor sales be less than fifty percent of an establishment's total revenue. The law went into effect July first and forced Caldwell's to close, same as two other places."

Shelby absorbed the ramifications. "Mike's a real-estate developer. He'd hate to have an investment lose revenue."

"Exactly. Your dad was the deciding vote. So Mike's threatened to sue if your dad touches the balloon."

Shelby could picture Mr. Thornburg's anger at having to close a profitable bar. Her dad could also be stubborn, especially if he thought he was working in the town's best interests. "Sounds complicated."

"Neither will back down and it's far too late for the city to sponsor another balloon. We'll have no balloon in our own race. We're sick over it. It's embarrassing."

Mrs. James shuddered as if she'd had a visible

chill. "The entry fees for the state race are nonrefundable. Mike insisted your dad reimburse the town and your dad refused. They've always represented Beaumont. We want our balloon and our best friends back. Try, will you?"

Beaumont was a close-knit community, and Shelby imagined everyone felt caught in the middle. Perhaps that was another reason why her parents hadn't told her any of this. Or about Luke's homecoming. Shelby stacked the three boxes onto her arm, shaking her head at Mrs. James's offer of a shopping bag.

"I don't know what I can do. I'll try. But no promises."

Mrs. James picked up her magazine and fanned herself. "Missouri mules and fools, both of those men. You make any progress and I'll give you free cookies for life."

"I'll talk to Dad." *And* figure out why he hadn't told her. "I can't believe he or Mr. Thornburg would deliberately hurt the town's reputation."

"Those two were the reasons we started our race. People come from all over the country. How can we host it and not have our own entry?"

With a sympathetic smile, Shelby turned for the door, the cookie boxes now balanced in both arms from chest to chin. The doorbell jangled, and Shelby paused. She peered around the stack so she didn't plow into the incoming customers.

A curly-haired brunette girl whose hair had been

tamed into pigtails raced into the store about the same time as an arm covered in soft dark hairs pushed the door inward and held it fully open. "I beat you fair and square!" the child squealed with delight.

Déjà vu washed over Shelby. While the hand was twelve years older, the shape remained similar. She recognized the faded scar on the forearm—she'd caused it when she'd accidentally crashed her bike into his.

"Mrs. James, I won! I finally won!" Realizing someone else was standing in the store, the girl gazed at Shelby with an expectant anticipation. Shelby noted the child had Maren's perky bow lips and Luke's deep brown eyes.

"Hi," Shelby said, her feet rooted as the six-foot frame of Luke Thornburg stepped inside. Her photographer's eye assessed him. He'd filled out—like her, he'd aged and lost his gangly teen awkwardness— but the same dark blond hair swooped away from his forehead. His face registered a mixture of shock and surprise, and his full eyebrows lifted.

They'd once been so in sync, and she knew her expression mirrored his, complete with the small O shape her lips made. She closed her mouth and schooled her features into a neutral expression, a requirement for someone who saw life through the camera lens—observing the action but not taking part.

"Shelby." Luke's mouth formed her name as if

more than a decade hadn't passed, and a sliver of bittersweet longing for lost dreams stabbed into her heart. She ignored the pulse of adrenaline running in her veins.

She'd been in far trickier situations, like dangling off a cliff in the Front Range of the Rockies, but those instances hadn't involved facing her former best friend and first lover—the one who'd declared in emails he wanted to marry you.

Until he hadn't.

"Luke." They stood almost eye-to-eye and Shelby drank him in. His chambray, button-down shirt was tucked easily into the waistband of his leather-belted jeans, the rolled-up sleeves of the shirt the epitome of casual fall fashion.

He noticed her midnight blue highlights. "I like the hair."

"Dad?" Anna—that was her name, Shelby's parents had sent her a scan of the birth announcement six years ago—tugged on Luke's hand. Her emotions a roller coaster, Shelby was grateful for the interruption.

"Let's get you a cookie, sweetie." Mrs. James led Luke's daughter toward the display case. "What's your pleasure? I made giant sprinkle cookies this morning and I know how much you love them."

Unlike Anna, Luke didn't move. Instead, his brow creased and he studied her in that thoughtful way he always had, as if he could peer inside her soul and see something no one else could. The idea he might still be able to sense her deepest secrets bothered Shelby, and she held the boxes aloft as a shield.

"You look well, Shelby."

"So do you." The truth slipped out—where was the age-thirty dad-bod flab? Why couldn't his blond locks be thinning, his hairline receding? But no. He looked as gorgeous and fit as ever. She'd have to maneuver past him to reach the door, and escape was a necessity. "Got to go—good seeing you. Haven't even made it home yet. We'll catch up later."

Breezy, friendly words, said like "How are you?" with no expectation of any real answer.

Luke's gaze pinned her like an arrow hitting the bull's-eye. "Promise?"

"I gave up pinkie swears." As the barb hit home, he frowned, and she stepped purposely toward the exit. "I'll be busy with Dad. I'm leaving Monday. Must get these there before tea. Nice seeing you."

"Shelby—"

A myriad stream of emotions—everything from sadness to anger to longing and desire—threatened to burst forth and betray her. She always imagined their next meeting being something she could control. She'd be calm. Sophisticated. Flick her hair as if she didn't have a care in the world. Not appear road-worn and carrying cookies. And there was no point in re-hashing the past, not when she'd load up her car and drive away Monday morning. She cut their conversation short with a "Got to go. Enjoy your cookies!"

She tried to sweep past him, but because the store was tiny and its few tables were strategically placed against the wall, the layout forced Shelby close enough to smell his aftershave—sage with a hint of sandalwood and musk, so very him. Once she'd run across a similar fragrance in a market in Marrakesh, and it had made her think of him and the childhood friendship they'd lost by believing they could make it more.

She'd left the market and headed back to her hotel, where she'd used the action of sending photos to her editor as a way to put both the market and Luke in the rearview mirror. Later, when Shelby had climbed on a flight for Lake Victoria and the Kenyan shoreline that evening, she pretended she'd left it all behind.

But clearly, she hadn't.

Today, the queen of leaving fled the cookie shop at a nonchalant pace. She balanced the boxes like precious cargo as she waited for a car to pass before crossing over the brick cobblestones, leaving behind wonderful aromas of baked goods and Luke. She refused to look back.

As a newer version of the same model car he'd ridden shotgun in throughout high school drove away, Luke forced himself to turn from the window. Shelby was back. A short visit—not quite four full days—

but after years of never expecting to see her again, running into her at the cookie store had caught him by complete surprise. It was also clear she couldn't wait to get away from him.

He didn't blame her, despite her actions being a punch to his gut.

Luke exhaled deeply and watched Anna pick out cookies. Despite Shelby's longer hair, now streaked with blue, he'd recognize her anywhere—same oval face with the pretty smile. Same bright hazel eyes with some flecks of gold. Same tug on his heart. She'd been his best friend, closest confidante and love of his life. Now they were worse than strangers.

Luke shook away the disquieting thought and focused on his daughter, the best thing to come from his and Maren's marriage. Anna excitedly pointed at this and that, and when Mrs. James caught his eye, she passed no judgment on Luke's encounter with Shelby. Instead, she went back to helping Anna with the task of picking out six different cookies.

"I see you chose a sprinkle one," he said as Anna finally decided on her half dozen.

Anna pointed to the case, where trays of cookies beckoned. "I also got a snickerdoodle, and a chocolate-chip—that's for you—and a fudge brownie one, a peanut-butter one for Grandpa and a sugar cookie for Grandma."

"They'll love you for thinking of them." That was his daughter, the kindest and sweetest person he knew and someone who always thought of others first. The other day she'd given out stickers to everyone in her kindergarten class "just because."

"I put together an assortment for Shelby, too." Mrs. James folded the bag so the top closed. "She hadn't heard about the fight."

"No?" He'd been living with the fallout.

Mrs. James handed the bag to Luke, who dangled the edges between his fingers. "I told her the town hopes your dad and John work through this. *Playgroup* needs to fly. I asked her if she still flew, but she didn't answer."

Luke knew Shelby would never let any certifications expire. Not after working so hard to get them.

"I like balloons," Anna interrupted. She had crumbs stuck on her lips, and Luke removed a napkin from the silver dispenser, handed it to her and pointed to her face. Anna dabbed until Luke's nod told her she'd wiped off all the cookie particles. "Remember, Dad? The fair lady twisted a turtle bracelet from a green one."

"Not those kinds of balloons," Luke corrected gently as he handed Mrs. James a ten-dollar bill. "The ones that go up in the air. Like Grandpa's. Like the time we went to the balloon glow. Remember how all the balloons were lit up like Chinese lanterns?"

"Ooh, those were pretty," Anna said. "Are we going again?"

"Of course." Even if *Playgroup* wasn't there.

Mrs. James handed Luke his change. "So is your festival booth ready to set up?"

Luke put the coins in the pocket. "Yes. But our booth and theirs won't be side by side like before. A quilter or something is between." He turned to his daughter. "You ready, Anna Banana?" He moved toward the door.

"Last one there's a rotten egg," Anna called.

"Not this time." He didn't feel like racing. Not after seeing Shelby.

"Aw, Dad," Anna protested.

"Do you want me to crumble the cookies?" A better excuse than reminding her that a few seconds ago she'd protested she was "too big." She'd already grown and changed, developing daily into her own independent young person.

Hearing Anna's "no," Luke winked at Mrs. James and held the door open for his daughter. "Let's go."

They stepped outside and began to walk to his parents' house so she could deliver the cookies. It took two seconds before Anna began skipping her way down the brick sidewalk and pulling ahead of him.

Rather than calling her back, he admired her verve and energy. She'd been three when Maren died. To give Anna as much of a normal childhood as possible following the loss of her mom, Luke had remained in their home in Cincinnati, near Maren's parents. Anna knew her mommy was in heaven and missed her, but his daughter was proof of resilence and the power of new memories. Anna was growing up, ready to grasp the brass ring with both hands. When Maren's parents had announced they were moving to Florida, Luke had used the opportunity to return to Beaumont on August first. So far, Anna loved Luke's hometown. She'd even led him through her kindergarten classroom during open house a few weeks ago, introducing him to the new friends she chattered about constantly. He watched as she bounded ahead, knowing the way, asserting some independence yet still safe with her dad right behind her.

She'd reached the wrought-iron fence surrounding the postage-stamp lawn of the Blanchette Inn, and as Luke passed by, habit had him glancing at the wide front porch. He noted that the ever-present, large green wreaths adorning the polished-wood, double front doors were displaying hot-air-balloon ornaments. Mrs. Bien made each month's wreath herself, and long ago he and Shelby had helped.

Habit meant Luke craned his neck toward the third-floor balcony. How many times had Shelby and he sat up there cross-legged? They'd watched the tourists walk by below, counted the boats out on the river and talked of all their hopes and dreams. To this day Luke couldn't pinpoint why he'd listened to Maren. What made him not recognize the snake in the garden until far too late? By then, though, her illness and Anna had kept him with her. He couldn't bear to be separated from his daughter, and he never would have tried to take her from her mother.

Moving to Beaumont was a second chance. A do-over of sorts.

And now he'd seen Shelby and everything that had happened, all the anguish and mistakes, had come rushing back.

The inn behind them, Anna bounced through the open gate of the next brick building and ran up the sidewalk leading to the large three-story Federal-style house where Luke had grown up. While his dad had acquired an extensive real-estate portfolio of houses and commercial buildings, his mother liked living on Main Street, next to her best friend.

The front two rooms of the first floor also held Luke's mom's business. Wall shelves filled with homemade specialty soaps and body scrubs lined the perimeter. Specialty candles and other products his mom accepted on consignment could be found on the round tables scattered throughout. He noticed a new display of pumpkin-scented candles, which would be a top seller during October.

Anna retrieved the bag from him and rushed her way up to the counter. "Grandma, I brought you a cookie!"

Luke followed leisurely, watching as his mom finished ringing up a customer before giving Anna her full attention. She bent to give her granddaughter a hug and squealed over how sugar cookies were her favorite. She took a big bite and said, "Yummy. Thank you." And then she added, "Do you have homework?"

Anna shook her head enough to make Luke dizzy. "No. We're off tomorrow because of the festival."

"Really?" Luke's mom arched an eyebrow. "You're not pulling my leg?"

"Uh-uh." Anna's curly pigtails jiggled as she laughed. "But don't worry. I will read. We checked out books at the school library today and I got two chapter books."

"Chapter books already. My, my."

Anna nodded. "They aren't big chapters, but that's okay because I can figure them out. Mrs. Lewis says I'm a good reader."

"Yes, you are." The bell tinkled as the customer left the shop. His mom gestured with her partially eaten cookie and pointed to the bag in Anna's possession. "Why don't you take these cookies in to Grandpa? I bet he's hungry. You did bring him one, didn't you?"

"Of course. I would never forget Grandpa. Grandpa," Anna called, disappearing through the doorway behind the counter and into the family section of the house.

Luke picked up a bar of his mother's famous lemon-scented soap. He felt rather than saw his mother tilt her head—she was studying him, as if she knew something was wrong. How did mothers do that? "I haven't seen that look since you were little and thought you saw Casper," she said. "What's wrong?"

Luke bristled with mock indignation. "Hey, the apparition was real. This building is well over two hundred years old. Something paranormal could have made that stuff fall off the shelf."

She shook her head. "While other buildings on this street are haunted, this one's not. You had the stuff too close to the edge and overloaded it. So let's concentrate on the look on your face. Something's up."

"We have a lot to do before the festival opens at four tomorrow." That was safe. But the next part wasn't. "And Dad's feud. How's it all going to work?"

His mom wiped her hands on her ruffled apron. "Same as always. Lots of arts and crafts being show-cased, fireworks tomorrow and Saturday night, and good food and entertainment all weekend. If the weatherman is to be believed, perfect weather. That means tourists and money to be made. Your dad will be civil or he'll answer to me, if that's what you're trying to get at."

Luke nodded. The entire length of South Main Street would become a pedestrian byway of booths, one of which included his mom's wares. In addition to the tourists staying at the inn and other B&Bs, the event would draw visitors from miles around.

She swiveled the credit-card machine. "I sense there's more, but I suppose that'll do for now. Stay for dinner. I've made enough beef Stroganoff to feed an army. Your sister's coming by, too. So it'll be family time."

"Okay, but we have to go home first."

"You should have moved in here, since you're here enough."

Luke had considered the idea briefly when he'd decided to return, but as he was used to having his own space, he'd politely rejected the offer. "Nah. You keep your sewing room. The apartment is perfect and Joe's Art Gallery downstairs is a quiet neighbor."

"Well, it's far better than living over that bar. If I'd known the drama that place would cause." His mom frowned as she made reference to Luke's first plan, which had been to claim the small apartment over Caldwell's. But the upstairs required a gut rehab, same as the bar area itself. Closing the place had been inevitable, not that his father would admit it. Still, his dad had given him carte blanche on the reno project, leaving it up to Luke to find a business plan the city would approve. "Mrs. James brought up the fact *Playgroup* is still grounded."

His mom sighed. "She means well and I'm doing my best. But your father is a proud man with a vacant building bleeding money. It might take him experiencing the consequences of not racing before he comes around."

Luke raked a hand through his hair. "That's too late. We have to do something now."

His mom straightened some brochures stacked on the counter. "I've already given your father my opinion. If you have an idea, take it up with him."

"I will." A group of customers entered and Luke welcomed the opportunity to follow in Anna's footsteps. But something made him pause in the doorway, and then, even though he'd sworn to himself he wouldn't say anything, he dropped his real bombshell. "By the way, Shelby's back in town for the weekend. I ran into her in the cookie store."

His mother's expression instantly softened. "Oh, Luke. Are you all right?"

No. Luke shrugged off the hurt. "It's fine. We were civil. She looks good, though. Really good."

The bell jangled, and another group of customers walked in. As his mother turned to greet them, Luke made his escape.

Chapter Two

Fewer than two minutes after leaving the cookie store, Shelby parked in an empty spot marked "resident," directly under the welcome shade of a 200-year-old oak tree.

Her parents' inn was an early 1800s structure—the stones forming the exterior walls and fireplaces had been chiseled by slave hands and carted to location by mule. Determined to remember and honor those whose forced labor had created the inn, her family had installed a marker on the inn's front lawn. Her dad had also tracked down descendants, who now held a family reunion every three years at the inn with all expenses paid. Beaumont had gone further by renaming some streets, paying reparations, installing a permanent exhibit at city hall and creating a scholarship fund. The town felt it was the least it could do.

Shelby stepped out and stretched. Even though it was too early for the oak to display any hints of the blazing reds, oranges and golds it showcased each October, the huge canopy provided nostalgic welcome. When she'd been in kindergarten—Anna's age—she and Luke used to build huge leaf piles and jump into them, scattering the leaves around only to rake them again and repeat the whole process.

Shelby shut the driver's door using the bottom of her foot—the cookie boxes filled both hands and her camera bag fit into the familiar dent in her shoulder. She'd retrieve her luggage later. Her mother's herb garden lined the back brick walkway—the large, round knee-high pots contained basil, mint, sage, tarragon and lemon balm. Each spring her mom put out the green-colored ceramic pots, and she'd store them once the growing season ended.

The walkway also wove through her mom's flower gardens, until the path through the deep back lot forked. One direction went around the side of the building to the front entrance the guests used. But Shelby climbed the back stairs to the wooden screened porch, where wind chimes tinkled in sporadic breeze. She elbowed the back doorbell. Her mom came into view, flicked the lace curtain and immediately threw open the door.

"Surprise!" Shelby greeted.

"Shelby! You're a day early! Oh, my goodness."

Her mom set down the laundry basket, took the cookie boxes from Shelby's hands and set them on top of the towels. Then she drew Shelby in for a huge hug. As long as she could remember, her mother always smelled like roses, and today didn't disappoint.

"It's my body lotion," her mom had once told a five-year-old Shelby. For the next two years, Shelby had to have her own bottle, until she'd reached second grade and required more independence.

In her teens, she had worn the smelly designer-knockoff perfumes and used the latest, trendy shampoo in an attempt to be cool. How naive she'd been. Now comfortable in her skin, Shelby used whatever the hotel stocked. It all worked, even if not as well as the soaps Mrs. Thornburg made.

The rose-scented hug worked its magic and the final vestiges of stress fled. To this day, Shelby hadn't found or experienced a better floral scent anywhere in the world.

They stepped apart and Shelby received a thorough once-over. "I swear every single time you come home you've changed. This time it's your hair. Are those colored highlights? They're fabulous."

"Midnight blue." Shelby held out the end of her ponytail so her mom could examine it. "I did this when I was in London. I mean, why not? It's subtle and just at the ends. Like it?"

"Yes. Yes, I do," her mom admitted with a laugh. "It looks great. I saw a girl at the supermarket and she was totally purple. Should I do something different?"

Except for hints of gray, her mom's hair was the same as in the wedding photo hanging in the third-floor hallway. "Don't change a thing. You're perfect the way you are." Shelby meant every word. "Is Dad here? I can't wait to see him."

Her mom tucked a stray strand behind her right ear. "He's out. The doctor might have his arm in a cast, but he refuses to sit still. He had some council meeting up at city hall, so Anthony drove him."

Anthony was their family's handyman. In his sixties, he'd been with the inn for thirty years. More than an employee, he'd become part of their family.

Based on what she'd learned at the cookie store, Shelby decided not to ask what her dad was doing at city hall. "I stopped for cookies. I figured you could serve them for tea. Some for us and some for the guests."

"We're definitely having a good year reservation-wise. The guests will love them. Thank you."

"You know me. I love sweets and I had a craving." Shelby set her camera bag on the kitchen counter. She reached into the cupboard for a tall glass, then filled it with water from the sink faucet and drank while her mom retrieved a serving platter. "I ate one already. Considering going back for number two." Shelby snagged a snickerdoodle. "Which I'll do now."

Her mom chuckled as Shelby bit into the cinnamon-flavored cookie and expressed a gastric "mmm" of delight.

"So good. Have one." Shelby gestured toward a box.

"Maybe later. Even looking at Jayne's cookies makes the pounds go straight to my hips."

"Mine, too, so I'll run on the Katy Trail tomorrow. And by the way, you look great." Her mom had a few more lines on her face than in the wedding photo, but looked fabulous. Even though she never stayed long, Shelby tried to see her parents at least once every three months.

Her mom moved chocolate-chip cookies to a serving platter. "You know I've tried to make them like this. While I know how Jayne James gets this extra scoop of batter on top, I can't seem to duplicate it."

"At least she can't make your coconut pie or your mile-high lemon meringue. Even I can't. My meringue falls every time." Shelby washed down the last of the cookie with sips of water. One nice thing about being home, Beaumont had some of the nation's best tap water. Shelby'd been in places where she hadn't dared to drink the water.

"If you stay long enough, I'll show you the secret." Her mom clasped her hands together in delight. "Thank you for surprising us. I'm so happy you made it in time for the start of the festival. We're gonna have so much fun."

"I can't believe how big it's gotten."

Shelby leaned her hip against the counter and

snagged a third cookie. Delicious peanut-butter flavor hit her tongue. "The sleepy festival I remember
now closes down the streets."

"It's really taken off these past two years. Whatever you do, don't spoil your dinner."

Shelby relished her mom's familiar chiding.
"Trust me, I'll still be hungry. I skipped lunch in
favor of some snack crackers I ate in the car."

Her mom appeared concerned. "Should I make
you something? A sandwich?"

"No, no. These cookies will hold me."

Her mom didn't appear convinced. "Let me know
if you change your mind. I plan to spoil you with
food so good you'll never leave."

But Shelby would go, despite her parents' wishes
otherwise. Pushing aside a twinge of guilt, she
switched subjects. "I heard about Dad and Mr. Thornburg from Mrs. James. Why didn't you tell me?"

Her mom sighed. "I figured it would be over by
now. You know about the ordinance?"

Shelby nodded.

Her mom twisted her hands into her apron. "It's a
mess. Mike took your dad's vote personally."

"But Dad was doing what was right."

"In his mind, yes. Cynthia and I don't know what
to do. It's not like they haven't had fights before.
They'll stew for a week, figure it out and things go
back to normal. It's like blowing off steam. This
one's different. Mike feels betrayed and your father
won't back down because he'll lose face."

"I'm sorry."

"Me, too. We were at Miller's shortly after Caldwell's shut its doors, and when they passed each other in the hallway…" Her mom shuddered. "We didn't want to worry you."

"You also forgot to mention Luke moved back. I ran into him in the store."

Her mom appeared sheepish, confirming she'd deliberately kept Shelby in the dark. "You weren't here and the feud kept me distracted."

Shelby let the excuse slide. Besides, she and Luke were ancient history, even if seeing him had made her heart miss a beat. "You and Mrs. Thornburg are okay, right?"

Her mom finished transferring the cookies and stored the rest. "Yes."

"After I take some pictures, I can help with the booth."

"Is your luggage still in the car?"

"Yeah. I'll get it now. Unless you need help?"

"I've got them. All the guests are checked in, the strawberry tarts for tomorrow's breakfast are baked and your dad and I made reservations for tonight. Call Miller's and tell them to change it to three people."

Shelby's mouth watered. "I can do that."

Her mom washed and dried her hands. "Perfect. I'm so glad you came for an extra day."

"Me, too." Shelby kissed her mom's cheek. She

knew it was hard on them to have their only child living so far away. "I love you and it's good to be home."

"We love you, too. It's not the same, flying to wherever you are, even though I loved Hawaii."

Once, after she'd finished an assignment to photograph scientists who studied volcanoes, Shelby had flown her parents out for a two-week vacation and tons of quality time in paradise.

"If you're sure you don't need me to do anything," Shelby offered again.

"No," her mom insisted. "Go unpack and don't forget to call Miller's."

After lifting the platter, her mom entered the inn's front parlors and Shelby heard the oohs and aahs of guests. Shelby returned to her car and removed the trash from today's drive. She carried two handfuls to the community dumpster located in the alley.

She was struggling with the heavy lid when a hand shot out and helped. "I see we had the same idea," Luke said.

"Thanks." She tossed in her items, and he followed with a white garbage bag. The heavy plastic lid thudded closed and reverberated. Luke stepped back and shoved his hands into his jeans. Shelby quickly jerked her gaze to his face.

"Everyone like the cookies?" he asked.

When he smiled, emotions long buried flared to life. Longing surfaced. She worked to keep her tone light. Neutral. "The guests were making appreciative noises when I came out for my luggage."

"That's great."

He fell into step beside her as if it hadn't been years since they'd walked side by side. Shelby decided she had two options. Be bitchy and add to the family feud, or be civil and neighborly and try to put the past behind her. Perhaps after this weekend, and after their dads stopped fighting, it wouldn't be so awkward if she came home for the holidays, something she'd purposely avoided.

As for the fact that he smelled divine and strode beside her like he belonged—irrelevant. The days when he'd been her whole world were long gone.

She lifted the tailgate, but Luke beat her to her luggage. His firm fingers wrapped around the handle. He set the suitcase on the concrete pad and made sure the wheels didn't start rolling before he grabbed the second, larger bag. "This it?"

"Yes. Normally I travel lighter, but I've been on the road for two months."

"You always said you planned to travel. I guess you got your wish. Where were you this time?"

"Stateside. I was in the Dakotas. Minnesota and Iowa."

"Your parents told mine how much they miss you. Proud of you, but missing you."

Shelby shoved aside the guilt. "Speaking of parents, I can't believe our dads aren't friends."

Luke closed the hatchback and the trunk clicked. "We thought we'd be friends forever."

"True." She frowned. How dare he bring up their

long-ago friendship? Especially as he'd been the one to end it by betraying her.

She dismissed their experience. "We were kids. They're adults. And what about *Playgroup*?"

Luke lifted her cases and carried them toward the house. "My dad told me, and I quote, he's 'not flying with that man.' He's dug in."

"They've been friends forty years. All this over having to serve more food?"

"It's a bit more," Luke said.

They reached the bench underneath the old oak tree. Shelby pointed. "I have a few minutes. Tell me." She sat on the wrought iron and patted the spot next to her. She ignored the familiarity of the movement. How many times had she asked Luke to sit with her here?

Luke set her suitcases next to her and sat on the opposite end, his knees about a foot away. Long fingers rubbed the tops of jean-covered thighs, calling attention to how fit he was. "I always said I wanted to run my own business."

He had. "Which is why I was surprised when my parents told me you became a lawyer."

"Was a lawyer," he corrected, and Shelby experienced a surprised jolt. "I left that behind when I left Ohio. Do you ever remember me dreaming of being a lawyer?"

"It's been so long," Shelby hedged, knowing the answer was no. At age six, he'd been the one to help her with her lemonade stand—they'd raised over one hundred dollars for charity after he'd taken over. She'd made the lemonade and popcorn—he'd built the stand and done the marketing and selling.

"I believe we declared we'd live forever side by side, with me running my mom's shop and you running the inn."

The memory created twinges of regret. "We were kids with silly kid dreams." She waved her hand as if shooing away a fly. "And you were always terrible at making soap."

"Still am," Luke admitted with a rueful laugh. "My sister's taking over. Maren's father was a lawyer, and it seemed like a natural path."

"It's logical you'd work to make her happy." Shelby pushed aside the bitterness. His betrayal shouldn't still resonate, but it did. She'd loved him with all her heart. But they weren't meant to be. If they had been, they wouldn't have fallen apart so quickly. Maybe seeing him this weekend would finally allow her to fully let go.

"After Maren died, I did some self-assessment." Luke fidgeted on the bench and rubbed the top of the denim covering his thigh. "I missed Beaumont. This is home. My dad bought Caldwell's for me."

Her forehead creased. "You wanted to own a bar?"

"No. But I wanted to come home. Now the bar's closing because of the new city ordinance and it has accelerated the timeline of my figuring things out. A closed building is not an asset. You can hear my dad saying that, can't you?" His lips puckered wryly and he shrugged.

"I can." She watched as a monarch butterfly flitted and landed on the full-bloom dahlias to the right of the bench. Seemingly without a care in the world, the creature opened and closed its wings. "I'm sorry."

He jerked a hand through his hair, something he'd always done when exasperated. "You don't need to apologize. You have nothing to be sorry for. And I hate that you and I aren't friends."

The butterfly flew off and Shelby's nerves heightened. He wasn't talking about Caldwell's. "We're different people in different worlds. What's important is mending the rift between our dads."

"I'd like us to be friends as well."

Shelby stretched her fingers. To her impressionable heart, Luke's rejection had stung. He'd started dating Maren when Shelby had been in Wyoming. But for him to not tell her—to hear it from Maren, of all people... "I know it sounds harsh, but I'm leaving in a few days. We don't have to rehash what once was when the future results will be the same. I don't live here anymore. You do."

She was no longer a small-town teenager dealing with the high of a huge, wondrous new love and the crashing anguish of heartbreak. Even if she felt like a flittering butterfly when around Luke, any relationship, even one as simple as being friends, was doomed to the same time and distance issues as before.

"My job is fulfilling and I love traveling," she continued, perhaps to convince herself as much as him. "Mastering the camera freed me to find myself and see the world."

In essence, photography had provided Shelby the perfect escape, and she'd run fast and far away.

Luke clasped his hands. Released them. "I liked the story you did on the blind climber who was bungee-jumping into all the great gorges."

She'd conquered one of her greatest fears by jumping into one of the gorges herself. "That was a fun assignment. I've met so many interesting people." But she never stayed. She entered their orbit and cycled out. His words sunk in. "You followed my career?"

"We were friends. Despite what happened, it didn't mean I wasn't interested in your success. You followed your dreams."

Once, he'd been her dream. A raw, uncomfortable twinge brought doubts to the surface. Many times, in the early days, she'd caught herself ready to contact Luke and share her latest adventures. Then she would remember how Maren had called her to apologize for seducing Luke. Shelby had told Maren she'd forgiven her—a lie. There was more, but Shelby refused to relive it. She'd managed to keep Luke and her hometown firmly in the rearview mirror. She was a big-city girl now. Happy.

She stood abruptly, bumping into her luggage. "I'll see if there's anything I can do on my end to soften my dad. But I know he won't back down from doing his job."

"Okay. Fair." Luke leaned forward, but remained seated. "I've been working on a new business plan and hope to get the permits soon. That might help."

Asking about his project would signal interest, and she refused to tumble down the rabbit hole. "Even if you reopen, someone has to fly *Playgroup* two weekends from now."

His gaze locked on to hers. "What about you?"

A flutter of panic mixed with excitement and Shelby took a step back. "I'm not flying *Playgroup*." Although she could. She'd passed her biennial flight review within the last nine months, since her photography work often took her up in the air for shots drones couldn't get.

"Why not? You've flown her before."

Where had he gotten this idea? *Mrs. James.* Shelby inhaled a calming breath. "That doesn't mean I should do it now."

He rose. "Give me a good reason you can't. You pilot. I'll crew. We can leave our dads out of it. Come on, Shelby. It's for the town. Our families. My daughter. The common good. The entry fee is already paid. What do you say? One more L-and-S adventure before you go jetting off again?"

L&S Adventures. Her mom had photo albums full of them. The volumes sat on a shelf upstairs.

A long pause, bordering on awkward, ensued. She couldn't get involved with him. Already she sensed a spark, a flicker of chemistry. Neither could be allowed to ignite. "I sympathize, but I didn't come here to fly."

Although a deep-down impulse urged her to do just that, to experience the rush of controlling a hot-air balloon. She loved being up in the sky, floating over the landscape while the heat from the burners mixed with the cooler air surrounding the basket.

"When's your next assignment?"

"A month away. But I'm driving back to Seattle with a few planned stops along the way to finish my current series."

"So there's nothing calling you back immediately? No cat? Boyfriend?"

She thought of her dusty ficus. "No. But I haven't seen my apartment in forever."

He reached for her but dropped his hand. "You probably don't even have food in your fridge."

Busted. She cleaned out the appliance before each trip, not that it ever contained anything more substantial than take-out containers or frozen meals.

"Work with me," Luke urged. "Stay. We can fly together. Saving the town? That'll be a bonus."

When she hesitated, he said, "We have a few practices, stand the balloon up at the glow, race and save the town pride. You go home being a hero and you'll spend extra time with your parents, which will make them happy. You'll still have two weeks to drive back. I have access to *Playgroup*. What do you say?"

Luke could sell ice in the frozen tundra. His wicked and engaging smile had always convinced her to participate in each and every one of his seemingly hare-brained schemes, which, 99.9 percent of the time, had not only worked out well, but had also far exceeded their wildest expectations. The man had more good ideas up his sleeve than common sense, which he also had in spades.

She grabbed the handles of her rolling suitcases. "I've got to get inside."

Luke nodded, the movement swift and easy. "I'll touch base with you tomorrow. You know Anna's ready to pull some plastic ducks out of your family's duck pond."

Luke strode off. Shelby remained rooted. Her photographer's eye caught everything. He didn't lumber or shuffle, or step gawkily as if he had a rock in his shoe. Nor did he move stealthily like a cat or bound over the pavement like an excited puppy. He had the fluidity of a calm stream on a relaxing fall day. She sighed.

Despite how he'd destroyed her, he remained the standard by which she judged all other men. She pivoted, and behind her, she heard the clang of the metal latch of the gate in the privacy fence between their properties as it opened and closed.

"There you are," her mom said as Shelby brought her luggage inside. If her mom had seen Shelby sitting outside with Luke, she thankfully didn't bring it up.

"Do I have time for a short nap?" Shelby asked, suddenly drained.

"Of course. Dinner's at seven."

Shelby glanced at her watch. "Perfect."

She opened the dumbwaiter, set her luggage inside, sent everything up to the third floor and took the back stairs two at a time while making the phone call to Miller's.

"Of course," Mrs. Miller told her, "we have room and can't wait to see you. It's been too long."

Shelby shoved her phone into her pocket, retrieved her luggage and carried it to a bedroom that had remained almost unchanged as the day she'd first left. While the antique canopy double bed had a new comforter, the tiny rosebud wallpaper was as old as she was. Framed prints of her photographs covered spots where posters once hung. She approached the 200-plus-year-old fireplace, which had been converted to gas in the 1990s. Her favorite stuffed animal sat in the middle of an ornate mantel covered with decorative trinkets. She lifted the lid of the Swiss-chalet music box she'd purchased in one of Main Street's antique shops. The waterwheel in the lower right began turning and the tinkling notes of "Edelweiss" burst forth. Seven notes in, she snapped the lid closed. Luke had convinced her to save up and buy it, and even after everything that had happened, and how it reminded her of him, she loved the box too much to give it away.

The corner of the mattress gave as she perched on

the edge. She caught her reflection in the oval mirror attached to the white vanity, part of the bedroom set that had been her Christmas present at age five. Then, she'd believed fairy tales came true. Luke was a prince and she a princess. A tomboy princess, but a princess nonetheless.

Then she'd learned *Grimms' Fairy Tales* were actually a series of dark concoctions meant to scare and terrorize children. She rose and went to her closet. She tugged on the metal chain to turn on the overhead light, and reached up to grab a small lockbox. She set the carved wooden box on the bedspread. Went to her camera bag and removed a key chain. The smallest key fit the lock. The black hinges sprang open, and Shelby dug under a few papers to remove a rubber-banded stack of photos. She flipped through them, finally finding a specific set. She fanned out the pictures of the balloon race the fall of her senior year of high school. *Playgroup* had won, to the town's delight.

Everyone looked so happy. There was the photo of the group inflating the envelope and another launching *Playgroup* into the air. Another one was of the entire group posing with the trophy. Yet another was of she and Luke mugging for the camera. She remembered the day and the participant dinner vividly, for it was the night she and Luke had slow-danced romantically for the first time. He'd held her tightly in his arms, her head nestled against his chest. Later, he'd asked her to be his girlfriend and go to homecoming with him. Three words summed up the night in her memory: Best. Night. Ever.

She fingered the photo showing her with her brown hair up in a ponytail, retainer in her mouth on full display in her big smile. By Christmas, she'd only had to wear the retainer at night. Back before spring of senior year, she'd never cared about appearances because she and Luke had been geeky together.

She stared at Luke's image. No, he was never geeky. Tall, relaxed, popular, kind and handsome were all better descriptors. They'd been each other's firsts in so many things. She sighed. He could have provided closure by telling her he wanted to see other people, or that his feelings had changed. His cheating had made the breakup even worse.

She picked up another photo and studied the happy faces of her parents and the Thornburgs. Over the years she'd seen even more victory pictures like these. Now, unless she piloted the balloon, their families wouldn't even participate. Disappointing everyone seemed so wrong.

She'd missed out on so much these past twelve years—a loss that was more acute whenever she returned home. Was that why she never stayed long? Was remaining on the road her way of proving she didn't miss Beaumont and the memories it contained?

As for Luke, why did her heart still give a little jump, as if it skipped a beat? She'd experienced more than a flutter of interest. She could be forgiven for not being immune to how well he'd aged. Thirty had nothing on him except for making him an attractive man.

Like old times, she'd sat on the bench with him. Wistfulness for the past, she decided. That was all this onset of melancholy was. She picked up the picture of her and Luke and their families. Luke's sister, Lisa, was in the shot with her husband, Carl. They'd been newlyweds for not even a month, choosing to marry a few weekends before the fall festival.

She had never fully explained why she'd avoided Luke, simply telling her parents they'd chosen different things and broken up. She'd hidden her true feelings by going straight from her summer photo experience to Seattle for college, and her parents had brought her belongings to her. Luke had followed Maren to Ohio. When Shelby visited Beaumont, by tacit, unspoken agreement, her mom and dad kept her up-to-date on the life of their best friends' son but they never levied an opinion or pried. They'd trusted her. Believed in her goals and supported her. Figured she'd tell them when she was ready, and since she didn't visit that much, they also didn't want to scare her away. Hence why they hadn't told her the latest, that he was back.

Boba, the inn's resident blue point Siamese cat, entered, weaving her way through furniture legs before rubbing her face against the smaller suitcase. The five-year-old cat hopped on the bed, kneaded the blanket and settled down for a nap. Shelby scratched Boba behind her soft gray ears, eliciting a brief purr. Then Shelby took one last look at the photo.

If she piloted the balloon, maybe she'd prove to herself—once and for all—she wasn't carrying some ridiculous childhood torch for a man who'd cared so little. She'd be able to rip off the fantasy blinders of Luke as being her soul mate—the reason all other men she met paled in comparison. She'd *truly* move on.

She locked the photographs away, returned the box to the closet and turned out the light. Too keyed up, she walked to the third-floor balcony and stepped out. Late-afternoon sun from behind the inn cast shadows on the street below. Visible over the tops of the buildings across the street, the sun made the Missouri River shimmer in ever-changing hues.

She heard a girl's shout and saw Anna skip out the front gate of her grandparents' house as she yelled, "Race you home!"

Luke, following leisurely, called out, "Don't get too far ahead," and they turned and went south, down the brick sidewalk until they disappeared from view under a thick canopy of tree branches still covered with leaves.

They didn't live next door? Shelby curled her fingers around the railing as something tugged deep inside her heart. The church bell chimed five, and down below, Main Street shops began to close. Sadie Hall came out of the bookstore and brought a rolling cart inside; she owned the shop with her mom.

Mrs. Coil retrieved the chalkboard sign advertising twenty percent off the jewelry in her shop. Mr. Collins watered his petunias in the two planters outside the double front door of the haberdashery. Shelby noted everything had changed, and yet somehow stayed the same. Nostalgia tugged, and some of the earlier tension she'd washed off during her mom's big hug crept back, arriving with a push-pull of swirling emotions Shelby didn't trust herself to decipher.

Despite the above-average heat, she shivered, so she went back inside, climbed into bed and drew the covers up to her nose. Shelby couldn't risk her heart. Not again. She wasn't going to fly *Playgroup*, not when doing so would put her into close proximity to Luke. He and the town would have to come up with something else.

Chapter Three

One thing about spending the night in her child-hood bedroom—Shelby always awoke refreshed. The next morning, after a divine meal at Miller's Grill, her eyes fluttered open after a solid, dreamless night's sleep. She reached for her cell phone, shift-ing on the firm mattress covered with soft, scented sheets. She'd slept everywhere from inside a cold tent at Everest's base camp to a humidity-drenched ham-mock draped with mosquito netting in the rainforest. She'd stayed two nights in an over-the-water bunga-low in Bora Bora and once in a suite at the Savoy Hotel in London, the pinnacle of high-end luxury.

But to quote Dorothy from *The Wizard of Oz*, there was no place like home. However, unlike Dor-othy, Shelby loved the yellow brick road and its adventures even more than the redbrick cobblestones and sidewalks of the Beaumont historic district. This bedroom—as wonderful and comfortable as it was—represented her past. Visiting acted like putting a battery on its charger. She reenergized and readied for the next adventure.

Bright morning sun peeked around frilly curtain edges, so Shelby changed into exercise clothes and laced up tennis shoes. Outside, she discovered the morning was positively perfect. Missouri summers could be unbearable, but early fall meant midday temperatures in the low eighties. She jogged down the alley, glancing quickly into the Thornburgs' backyard as she ran by. No one stirred. She continued on, making a left onto the sidewalk of First Street before darting across Main Street and then River Road. In a rails-to-trails initiative, Missouri had converted 240 miles of the former Missouri-Kansas-Texas line. Nicknamed the KT, or Katy, the trail crisscrossed most of the state, and the riverfront park contained one of 26 trailheads. Deciding to head south, she jogged past a fully restored depot.

Well-packed gravel crunched as she ran and she tried to keep the memories from encroaching. Long ago she and Luke used to take their bikes and ride all the way down to the next town and back. They'd pool their money to split sodas and ice cream. Shoving aside the memory, Shelby raised the volume of her music and pushed herself harder.

She found her dad in the kitchen when she returned, and after a quick shower, joined him at the table. With his good arm, he lifted his fork. "Enjoy your run?"

"It was great." Shelby bit into a strawberry tart and ripe berry flavor burst over her tongue. She followed with a sip of her mom's freshly squeezed orange juice. "What can I help with today?"

"Nothing. Anthony and I have the booth ready to go."

"Okay." She pushed aside the slight disappointment and decided to press a little. If she could get her dad and Luke's father back together, problem solved. "I had hoped to take pics of *Playgroup*. Are you sure you and Mr. Thornburg won't fly?"

Her dad's shoulders tensed. "No. He's being ridiculous."

"The building was an investment."

"He was going to close it for rehab, anyway." Her dad forked up more eggs. "He's being an ass."

"But *Playgroup*?" Shelby asked between bites. "I'd hoped to get those pics."

"It's in his storage center. Cast comes off Tuesday. I'd fly it myself if I could." Her dad lifted his arm. "But unless I get a court order, I'd be breaking and entering if I cut the lock off. I checked."

Shelby's hand froze, a strip of apple-smoked bacon dangling. "You're suing him?"

"Not yet."

Shelby hadn't realized the situation was this bad. No wonder Luke had approached her. "Everyone in town is upset."

"Yeah, I know." Her dad's face set into the rigid frown she knew from childhood that meant "no means no."

"They'll get over it," he growled. "I am." Having eaten with record speed, her dad rose to refill his plate. "He needs to apologize. He's got two weeks to come to his senses."

Shelby knew neither would give an inch.

So she let her dad change the subject. They talked about the Cardinals. Her travels. Her mom bustled in, carrying an empty platter. "The tarts were delicious," her dad said.

"They were," Shelby added. The trio made quick work of cleanup. Once the church clock chimed ten, residents and shopkeepers sprang into action. Tents and tent canopies began to pop up along Main Street.

Her parents brushed aside Shelby's offer to help with, as her mom said, "We've got this down to a science by now." With nothing specific to do, Shelby retrieved her camera, relying on her chosen vocation to fill the time.

With her finger on the shutter button, she captured the activity. One-handed, her dad pulled out tent poles. Anthony clipped them together and up went the tent. Sandbags secured the corner supports, and Anthony tied back the white canvas panels so three sides were open. Her dad filled two kiddie pools with a garden hose and her mom dumped in dozens of rubber ducks. Ducks of all sizes and colors bobbed along in a small current formed by the fish-tank pumps. Prizes included ten-inch stuffed animals, oversize plastic sunglasses, bottles of bubbles with wands and a plethora of swirled lollipops and Ring Pops. Shelby was in her element—chronicling everything, but not quite a part of anything. Just the way she liked it.

Shelby photographed everything, sending several jpegs to her editor straight from the camera's Wi-Fi connection. She and Jennifer were close, or as close as you could be with someone you saw in person a few times a year. But they talked all the time via phone or video conference, and Shelby considered her fifty-year-old editor a good friend.

With her family's duck-pond booth ready, Shelby stepped out into the middle of Main Street and took a wide shot looking north. She used leading lines, making the vanishing point far down the road, where everything seemed to converge almost dead center of the frame.

She flipped the camera vertically and captured the repetition of the storefront canopies lining Main Street, contrasting them with the historic brick buildings situated behind. She zoomed her lens and snapped Mrs. Clark's granddaughter, who was up on tiptoes tucking a book into the little free library outside her grandmother's bookstore.

Shelby turned south, sweeping her lens from left to right, until it focused on a sculpted torso clad in a fitted navy blue T-shirt. She lifted upward to catch Luke's profile. Unobserved, she took several shots as he supervised Anna, who was stacking soap into pyramids.

Anna noticed Shelby first, tugging on her dad's shirt hem while pointing in Shelby's direction. Then again, Shelby wasn't hard to notice; she was in the center of the road. After getting a go-ahead nod, Anna skipped in her direction. "Whatcha doing? Taking pictures? Can I see? I like photos. I use my dad's phone. I take pictures of flowers. I like flowers."

Shelby couldn't fault the child for her parentage, and Anna's enthusiasm was infectious. "You do, huh?"

"Flowers are pretty." Anna bounced and studied Shelby. "You're pretty."

"Why, thank you." Shelby had on jeans, a plain black T-shirt and tennis shoes. Her hair was up in a ponytail. "So are you."

"Can I see the pictures?" Anna asked again.

Shelby stood for an imperceptible second before moving into action. Anna was serious.

"Of course." Shelby turned the dial to preview mode, bent down and scrolled. "This is Main Street up by the bookstore."

"I spy Julia! She's still in preschool. I'm a year older than her." Shelby surmised Julia was the name of Mrs. Clark's granddaughter and Sadie's daughter.

"Her dad died. My mom died." As Shelby's stomach clenched, Anna pointed to the screen and thankfully moved on to the next photo. "Look, there's Jake the kitty."

"You have a good eye." Relieved, she enlarged that particular part of the photo. In one of few storefronts without a bright canvas canopy, a black-and-white cat was lying on its side on the ledge inside the front window. Jake sprawled between two mannequins, his white stomach exposed to all passersby as if he had no other cares than to sleep in the sun.

"Many people wouldn't have seen him," Shelby told Anna. "Watching foregrounds and backgrounds is important when taking pictures."

Anna squinted her eyes as if to peer closer. "Jake doesn't let many people pet him, but I can. What's a foreground?"

"It's the stuff in the front of the photo. The background is what you see in the back. This planter is in the foreground and Jake is way behind it in the background."

Anna pointed again. "Down the street there's a lamppost, but it's blurry."

"It's called selective focus. I made it that way. And yes, the lamppost is in the background."

Anna's gaze shifted from the LCD screen to Shelby. "You have a kitty, too. Boba." It came out

Bow-buh, with a heavy emphasis on the second syllable rather than the first.

"Boba is my mom and dad's kitty. I bet she lets you pet her, too."

Anna nodded vigorously, the bows in her hair catching the breeze. "And she sits in my lap." Anna's face scrunched up slightly. "Not lately. Grandma says we can't go visit like we used to. I like Mrs. Bien. She makes good pies."

She pronounced it *Bean* rather than *Bee-n*, but Shelby didn't correct her. The fact that a young child had been caught up in the two men's feud bothered Shelby greatly. "She does make good pies."

"Is Mrs. Bien your mom?" Anna asked. "You're lucky. I like her spaghetti. It's my favorite."

"She is my mom, and, yes, she makes good spaghetti."

As kindergartners do with a captive audience, Anna kept talking. "Once me and Grandma snuck over to the inn. I helped make biscuits. With the big rolling pin."

The rolling pin was as old as Shelby, but her mother refused to get another one.

Anna wiggled. "Grandma says we can't visit anymore. Not like we did."

Not liking the sound of that, Shelby scrolled to another frame. "This is you."

Anna leaned closer. "There's my dad."

"Where's your dad?" Luke strolled over to join them.

"In the photos that…"

Anna paused, curled her lip under and looked at Shelby for help. "You can call me Shelby," Shelby assured her.

"In Shelby's photos. See?" Anna used her finger to direct Luke's attention. "Show more, Shelby. Please?"

Highly aware of Luke being next to her, Shelby scrolled through the festival pictures. Luke's head came up when he finished viewing, and he arched an eyebrow. "Seems there's a few of me."

"You're part of Main Street," Shelby defended. "And photogenic. You always were."

"They're good pictures," he said, complimenting her.

"Thank you." Shelby was aware of the spike in her heart rate, which raced faster every time he came closer. It shouldn't. She was no longer a silly high schooler in love with her best friend. But tell that to her libido, as it strained to catch a whiff of sandalwood and sage. Her breath caught.

Anna gazed up at Shelby. "I wish I could take photos like you. Can you teach me?"

"Ah, pumpkin, Shelby's busy," Luke inserted quickly with an apologetic smile Shelby's direction. "Let's not bother her."

Shelby wasn't going to let Luke push her around, especially as Anna's lip quivered, creating the most crushed expression. Shelby had a soft heart for kids and a small chip on her shoulder. Minus Luke, her parents and her journalism teacher, few had believed she could turn her love for photography into a career. Shelby owed a great deal to the photographer who'd stayed at the inn after Luke had left town. Shelby always paid it forward. And what better time than the present?

"Tell you what. I have a few minutes. How about we walk around, down the block a bit and back. No farther than the church. I'll show you a few things. Will that work for you, Dad?" Shelby purposefully mimicked Luke's earlier movement and arched an eyebrow at him, as if daring him to say no.

"Can we, Dad? Can we?" Anna begged, putting her hand on his arm.

To avoid three being a crowd, Shelby said quickly, "Oh, your dad is busy helping with the booth. This is a girls' trip. You and me. We'll stay in your dad's sight so he doesn't have to worry."

"Go ahead," Luke conceded.

"Yay!" Anna hopped, and without giving Luke a chance to change his mind, Shelby turned and strolled down Main Street with Anna skipping along to her right. They walked past Luke's family booth, and out of the corner of her eye, she saw him rake a hand through his hair and shake his head before heading underneath the canopy.

Shelby took satisfaction in Luke's capitulation. In the past, she'd often let him lead and backed down. When he'd left, she'd realized the void she'd created by doing so.

She and Anna made their first stop in front of a clothing store.

"Okay, lesson one. You always do this." Shelby put the strap around Anna's neck. "You always wear the camera around your neck because if your hands slip, the camera hits you and not the ground. Hitting the ground is bad."

She'd once dropped an 800-dollar lens, but luckily cracked only the filter. "This lens is big and heavy. Here's how you hold it. Pointer finger here."

Anna soon held the camera correctly—with her right finger on the shutter release button and the rest wrapped around the body. Her left hand now supported both body and the 70-200 mm lens. It was a bit unwieldy for smaller hands. Shelby decided she'd bring a monopod next time she worked with Anna—an odd thought since Shelby was leaving town Monday.

"I'm going to tell you something my college professor told me."

Eyes wide, Anna stared over the top of the camera and waited.

"You're going to hear people tell you there are rules you must follow when composing photos. My professor said rules should be viewed more as suggestions."

Anna's brow wrinkled. Shelby simplified. "You're the photographer. You choose the picture. You decide."

Learning that had been a tough lesson. Her professor had used the example of Nat Fein's Pulitzer Prize winning photo. Shot in June 1948 at Yankee Stadium, Fein's photo was of a dying Babe Ruth's slightly hunched back, the number 3 clearly visible on his jersey, his hat in his left hand and the bat he was leaning on in his right. By shooting the photo this way, the viewer saw what Babe saw as he said goodbye: his team and his fans on their feet telling him how much they loved him.

So much for the rule about never taking photos from the back. Which meant Shelby made suggestions, but didn't criticize anything Anna composed.

"Can I show my dad my pictures?" Anna asked.

"Of course." They'd reached the end of the block, having walked in the opposite direction of the church. The Thornburg booth was about eight booths behind them, almost out of eyesight. She and Anna moseyed their way back, occasionally stopping to take one or two more photos before Shelby retrieved her camera and wrapped it around her neck. Along the way, she uploaded the photos to the cloud so she could share them later with Anna. Shelby's watch read 11:58 a.m., meaning it was probably Anna's lunchtime. Shelby's own stomach remained full from breakfast—she'd eaten far more than her typical grab-and-go fare.

Shelby kept a watchful gaze as Anna bounded ahead—skipping was clearly her preferred method of travel. Anna entered the booth and tugged her dad's shirt. Shelby couldn't hear their animated conversation, but Luke was standing outside the entrance when Shelby arrived. As he caught her gaze, he grinned, and her heart joined Anna in skipping.

"Anna tells me she learned a lot. You're a great teacher."

"Thank you." Shelby couldn't help but bask in the warmth of his smile, or long to trace the deep dimples surrounding his full lips. "She's a natural. I'll email a download link."

"Email's the same," he told her.

She stepped out of an incoming customer's way, which closed the space between them. "Give me until later tonight, although most likely sooner if I leave now." As her chest tightened with heightened awareness, she shifted her weight to prove she was ready to go. Exiting his magnetic presence became as essential as breathing.

He was a sexy, desirable man: from the scent of his aftershave, to the strong line of his jaw, and who could forget the delightful dimple in his chin. Desire and longing warred with common sense. A few more days and she'd be on the road. Luke would remain behind, as much part of the fabric of this historic town as those who'd come before him.

"Shelby! I thought I heard your voice! So good to see you!" Luke's mom wedged between them and embraced Shelby. "When did we see each other? A year ago? After Morocco? Look at you. Love the hair."

"Thanks," Shelby replied. "I arrived early."

"Good for you." Mrs. Thornburg reached forward and brushed a stray hair out of Shelby's face, as she had when Shelby had been a child. "Your mom never stops talking about you. She's so glad you're home, even if it's short."

Not to be left out, Anna chimed in. "I took pictures, Grandma."

Luke's mom gave Anna her full attention. "Did you?"

"Shelby taught me." Anna gave a small jump to put her more level with the adults, if only for a second.

"Here." Escape thwarted, Shelby turned on display. Luke lifted up Anna so she could see, and the hairs on Shelby's arm prickled from his close proximity.

"Anna, these are great," Cynthia declared. "Shelby, you're a good teacher."

"She's got a good eye," Shelby said, wanting to get out of the spotlight. While she wasn't facing Luke, she sensed him. Knew he was watching her.

"Hey, what's this? Why aren't we working? Oh. Hello, Shelby." Mr. Thornburg came into the tent from behind, cardboard box in hand. "This booth won't stock itself, you know."

"That's my cue," Shelby said, eager to flee. She smiled politely and edged toward the front of the booth.

Anna turned to her dad. "Dad, I'm hungry. Is it lunchtime?"

Called it, Shelby thought as she began to extricate herself.

"We have a tray of sandwiches inside in the fridge," Cynthia said. "Shelby, you eating with us?"

Shelby paused, aware of all the faces watching her. Mrs. Thornburg's reflected sincerity. Her husband scowled. Anna looked excited. Shelby couldn't read Luke, as he'd schooled his features into a mask. "Thanks for the offer, but I should see if my mom needs anything. I'll tell her you said hi."

Exiting, she speed-walked past the booth in between, where the occupants were hanging a queen-size, double-wedding-ring quilt. In the past, lunch would be at the inn, and the two families would flow back and forth, helping each other. The feud made things sad. The way Mr. Thornburg had glared had been unnerving.

Finding herself unneeded at their booth, she headed to her room and put away her camera. Before she opened her laptop, a text message from her editor pinged. Where are you? You didn't fill in the file info. What's going on? Jennifer demanded.

My hometown's fall festival, Shelby texted. Barely finished hitting Send, her cell rang with an incoming video call. Her editor's face filled the screen.

"That is the cutest street," Jennifer greeted without preamble. She was in her office, her vivid red blouse a perfect complement to her mocha skin. Out the window behind her, Shelby could see downtown

Seattle and, farther north, the spire of the Space Needle. "Tell me more."

"Hold on. Let me show you."

Shelby went to the third-floor balcony. She transposed the screen and panned so Jennifer could see the street below. Shelby switched the phone so her face appeared in the upper right corner. "The weather is perfect, so it's going to be great for business."

"Send me ten photos. I'll use them next week for a web-only feature. The festival's outdoors, so this fits. Besides, I'm curious. You don't talk about your hometown. It's historic, right?"

Shelby swore she had. "Yes. My family's inn is over two hundred years old. The festival is an annual event of arts-and-crafts booths and nightly entertainment. It's a huge moneymaker. People come from all over."

"Keep talking. We haven't featured a historic Midwestern town in ages. What else happens there?"

"A 5K race?"

Jennifer shook a head covered in black hair worn naturally. "I need more than a walk-run event. Leif's feature on Swedish hiking trails hit a huge snag. He's got a metatarsal stress fracture and can't hike for eight weeks."

"Ouch." Shelby wouldn't wish that on anyone.

Jennifer leaned back and put her fingertips together. "Tell me about it. What is it with people breaking things? Your dad? Leif? Anyway, I have a hole in the March issue and a fast-approaching press date. Our readers like all kinds of travel. Sell me on your hometown. If I assign you his spreads, your topic needs to be more than macramé."

Shelby's adrenaline spiked. Leif's feature was four spreads' worth of coverage, a coup for any photographer, especially the magazine's lone female. "It's more like painting. Soaps. Cookies. Wood carving. Quilting and knitting."

Her editor frowned. "Not enough. For web, yes. Print needs more. You'd write the text, too. And I need it in three weeks."

Shelby thought fast. If she got this assignment, both bylines would be hers. Normally her work accompanied someone else's story. While she'd had photos published in eight of the last twelve months, to be the month's featured photographer was a coveted accomplishment she'd not yet achieved. It would be nice to also use her English minor.

Her editor misinterpreted her silence. "You know this is also the cover, right? But if you have nothing, I need to find something else fast and—"

Shelby refused to lose this chance to shatter a glass ceiling. "There's an annual hot-air-balloon race."

Jennifer straightened and Shelby knew she'd caught her interest. "The town hosts a balloon race? A town that small? What is the population, like two thousand people?"

"Give or take and, yes, we do." Pride swelled. "It's a huge deal. My parents co-own a balloon and they enter ever year. They've even won."

Jennifer waved her hand in a rolling motion. "Keep talking."

Shelby zeroed in on a possible angle. "I'd focus on the small-town-togetherness aspect. Albuquerque, New Mexico, has over five hundred entrants. We top out at fifty. The state race has seventy and occurs next weekend. The town purposely put ours the weekend afterward so many out-of-town state competitors come to town and stay here the week in between. The racers often bring their bikes and ride the Katy. It's a rail-to-trail. The town's race also gives festival-goers reasons to come back two weeks later."

Jennifer nodded thoughtfully, picked up her Cross pen and made a few notations on a scratch pad. "I'm liking the small-town aspect and the idea of fifty balloons. Everyone always focuses on the big races. And we haven't covered the Katy Trail in my tenure." She made another note. "What else?"

"The balloons take off from the city park. People come from miles around. There's a balloon glow the night before where we inflate and light the balloons and people can walk between them." Shelby sent up a silent prayer for good weather.

"I'm liking this idea because of the personal connection of you and your parents. You could talk about the event from that angle."

"They aren't flying this year."

Jennifer appeared disappointed. "Leif had a personal narrative. I guess we can change it up, but…"

From the crease evident in her editor's forehead and the rapid twirling of her pen, Shelby sensed the opportunity slipping away. "Leif was hiking and photographing, right?"

Jennifer set down the pen. "Yes."

"I can fly the balloon."

Silence fell, and Boba began kneading her front paws into the fuzzy blanket covering the end of Shelby's bed. Shelby almost wondered if the connection had frozen until Jennifer said, "You can fly the balloon? I knew you were a pilot, but…"

Shelby's career relied on getting Leif's spreads, making her the magazine's first female to have the monthly feature "Yes. I can write a personal narrative on what it's like to race. There's a crew who helps get the balloon ready."

"Better." Her editor paused. "This is a huge opportunity for you. I'll have Elise rearrange your other assignments so you can stay in Missouri. Focus on making it as personal as possible."

Elise was Jennifer's assistant. Suddenly overwhelmed by the reality of what was happening, Shelby took a deep breath. Jennifer noticed. "I sense some hesitation."

"I should tell you who my crew is." Shelby came clean with her editor about Luke and the family feud.

"So, Luke," her editor said when Shelby finished. "The one you told me about when your tongue loosened following that extra glass of wine."

"That Luke," Shelby confirmed. "I'd understand if you decide to go with something else."

"Are you kidding?" Her editor brought her hands together in a silent clap. "It's even better. Leif planned on conquering the trails. His injury adds another obstacle to write about. You have perfect external and internal conflict. A conquering of your past. Self-realization, growth and working with your childhood sweetheart. Our readers will eat it up. And a family feud to boot? Extra drama. Don't bury the lead next time. I might have to come see the mythical Beaumont for myself."

"You're more than welcome. We're fully booked but there's always room for friends."

"I'll check my schedule. We editors don't get out often and it sounds fun." A beep sounded, and Jennifer glanced at her lower screen. "Have a conference call in five. We'll talk soon. But, Shelby, congrats. I'm excited about this. It's a great opportunity for you."

Jennifer disconnected, and Shelby tossed her phone onto the bed. Four spreads. The cover, with her name in 36-point lettering in the lower right corner. She could picture the headline: Shelby Bien Soars Beyond Small-town Life.

Her mind started contemplating potential shots. While she couldn't use a drone in the race because of temporary flight restrictions—nor would she, because of the potential danger to herself and all other balloons in the sky—she could, however, use a drone during practice. As a skilled drone pilot, she could get some cool aerial shots of the entire length of the envelope when it was lying in the grass before inflation. She could get a shot when *Playgroup* stood up. *Playgroup* was so pretty—the crown a solid orange surrounded by yellow triangles so the top looked like a sunburst.

Shelby removed a small notebook from her camera bag and began a list of potential shots. Good photographers planned everything, and then they let those plans fly out the window if something better appeared. Spontaneity was an important hallmark of photography. Once a black bear had ambled into the frame and the photographer she'd been with had refused to snap the photo because the assignment was a wide shot of a waterfall. The magazine had used Shelby's shots with the bear.

She stroked Boba's head, and the Siamese shifted so Shelby could scratch behind the cat's ears. Four spreads would put her on the same level as the magazine's elite male photographers.

All she had to do was fly *Playgroup*…with Luke.

Chapter Four

Perhaps it was the heavy weight off his mind—Shelby had said yes to flying *Playgroup*—that made Luke snooze his alarm and sleep in. When he crawled out of bed fifteen minutes later, he felt well-rested, as if the deep sleep had washed away some of his worries.

Yet, as he faced Saturday morning, other doubts had crept in. He wanted more than to help the town save face. Seeing Shelby yesterday had brought back all sorts of memories. Like how the summer before senior year he'd started noticing her as a woman. How her hand had fit in his once he'd finally dared to hold it. How their first kiss as teenagers had blown his mind. How his heart felt as if it would burst after they'd made love. How he'd missed her and wished she'd been in London with him to see all the sights. How, up until her emails slowed before stopping altogether, he'd spent every night writing her and staring at the photo in his wallet.

No point rehashing how their relationship had exploded in such a spectacular fashion, or the cruel words he'd thrown at her during their fight.

Words he now knew were unjustified. Maren... Luke shook his head. He'd been so blind. Foolish. After he'd discovered her cheating, they'd planned on divorcing. And then she'd gotten sick. Luke pushed aside the deceptions of his wife. All he had was the present.

He'd been handed a second chance.

He'd been surprised by Shelby's decision. When she'd found him at the festival, she'd kept it short. "I'll fly," she'd said. "I'm doing it as part of a magazine assignment featuring the town. We can talk details later." Then she'd handed him a business card with her cell-phone number and walked off. Her reasons smarted slightly, but Luke focused on the positive. He had two weeks to put things right.

Anna sat on a stool snugged up to the breakfast bar. She dipped her spoon into her Raisin Bran.

"Hey, pumpkin," he greeted, planting a kiss atop her head. "Sleep well?"

"Uh-huh." She turned a book page.

Anna still had the milk out, so he poured enough to cover the brown flakes in his own bowl before returning the carton to the refrigerator. He sat to Anna's right. Because she was absorbed in her book, he opened his phone and checked email. He had several unread messages, but only one sender caught his attention.

Shelby Bien.

For brief moment, his heart seized with the fear that she'd changed her mind, but the subject read Anna's photos, so he relaxed. Hi, Luke, she'd typed. Here's the link to where you can download Anna's photos. She did great. —S

Luke clicked the hyperlink and scrolled through a few thumbnails. Anna closed her book. "Shelby sent your pictures," he told her.

"Yay! Let me see." Anna scooted over and pointed to the first photo. "There's the flowers in the bucket." As they clicked through, Anna began to tell him about each picture, prefacing most of her descriptions with Shelby-said-to-do-this statements.

Shelby was a great teacher, Luke noted. Anna had captured life on Main Street, including the cat in the storefront window, the bookstore owner and Mrs. James and her famous chocolate-chip cookies. Anna had taken some photos of fence posts and other landscape features as well. "Shelby says foregrounds and backgrounds matter," Anna announced. "She told me that first."

"Well, you did a fabulous job."

"A photographer tells the story they want the viewers to see," Anna told him, clearly repeating something else Shelby had said. "I'm ready for my next lesson."

"We shouldn't bother her," Luke hedged. Shelby was already flying *Playgroup*. He didn't want her getting cold feet.

Anna put her bowl in the sink. "Don't worry, Dad. She said teaching me was fine. I asked her yesterday."

Of course Anna had. She might be wearing a pink nightgown with a unicorn on the front, but she was six going on sixteen. Ten years and she'd be asking for the car keys.

Luke reached over and ruffled her hair, laughing as he got an "I'm too big" as she tried to duck away. "You're never too big," he teased.

He'd been blessed. Knew how lucky he was. Anna had a big heart, was always doing random acts of kindness. She was generous, sweet and social, and she'd handled their move to Missouri with enthusiasm and excitement. He knew she missed her mom, but Anna's enthusiasm for Beaumont helped blunt the loss. They'd put a picture of Maren on the bookshelf, but it wasn't a shrine, for which he was grateful. Anna was also the type of kid who grasped life with both hands. She looked forward, not back.

The therapist he'd consulted said Anna was adjusting well. Luke sometimes envied his daughter. As the adult, he shouldered many mental burdens, including Maren's bombshell deathbed revelations. After years of therapy himself, he'd processed through the anger and the grief, but the guilt remained. His memories of Shelby remained as bittersweet as the day he'd made a pinkie swear to stay friends forever.

And now she was here.

He also carried the weight of revitalizing Caldwell's. Yesterday, the city building commissioner had approved his blueprints and issued a building permit. He could turbocharge the rehab starting Monday.

He had a vision. Caldwell's was about to become a makerspace, where artists and craftspeople could gather in a family-friendly venue. When he'd been a teenager, he'd loved helping Anthony build and repair things around the inn. Now, he planned to provide a place for members and patrons to work on everything from small welding projects to glass blowing to weaving and sculpture. In addition to a membership fee, artists could rent custom spaces to make items they could either sell at the festival or the local farmers' market, depending on the quantity. He could charge for classes, too. In addition to its benefits for the community and its culture, the ideas to make it work financially were endless.

Minus those in the building commissioner's office, he hadn't told anyone his plans, including members of his family. Even Mr. Bien didn't know—after all, the city council didn't review day-to-day operations of city departments. Luke would keep things under wraps until it was time to advertise his grand opening, He didn't want to jinx the process…and he wanted to do it on his own. Stand or fall. If he failed, he could return to law, even if practicing law didn't make him happy.

Luke stored Anna's photos in his cloud storage. "How about you go get dressed and, after I shower, we go see if Grandma needs any help? There's also a magic show. I know you don't want to miss that."

"Nope." Anna scampered off to her room.

After a shower and shave, he dressed in a baby blue polo shirt and a pair of khaki chino shorts—what every Midwestern dad wore—that fell about six inches above his knees. His phone case had space for his ID and credit card, and he shoved the apartment key into his right front pocket. Anna had on a pair of jean shorts, a floral T-shirt with bow ties on the sleeves, white tennis shoes and yellow socks with embroidered butterflies on the cuffs.

At the festival start time, Main Street was teeming with life. Vendors adjusted their canopies and curtains and restocked their booths. The smells of kettle corn, smoked turkey legs and barbequed pork steaks filled the air. A few clouds dared to sweep across the bright sky—high cirrus clouds spreading like wispy feathers.

Luke and Anna walked toward his mother's shop, and upon seeing her grandmother, Anna scampered ahead. Luke followed leisurely, his gaze tracking his daughter. She darted into the tent and his mom wrapped her in a hug. When he arrived, he gave his mom a kiss on the cheek. "Hey."

"Good morning," she said.

Luke watched as she restocked the displays. "You sold a lot yesterday."

"We did." His mom broke down an empty cardboard box. "Bodes well for today and tomorrow. What are your plans?"

"Magic show. Lunch. Maybe stop and check on Caldwell's. Naptime for Anna. More festival. Dinner. Fireworks."

His mom laughed. "Busy day."

"But here if you need me," Luke said. He glanced around, noting Anna stacking soap. "Have you seen Lisa?"

"Your sister's scheduled for noon."

"Perfect. Magic show's at eleven so I'll stop by afterward." Luke needed Lisa and her husband, Carl, to help crew *Playgroup*. They'd already volunteered, and with Shelby in, it was time to firm up plans. "I'll forward you the link to Anna's pictures so you can download them."

"Thanks. It was so nice of Shelby teach Anna. So how is she?" His mom dropped the question so nonchalantly that Luke did a quick double take. She meant Shelby.

"Fine."

His mom arched an eyebrow, putting Luke on the defensive. "We're friends. Sort of. Nothing more."

His mom remained silent and Luke filled the gap. "She's staying through the town race."

His mom finished storing the flattened cardboard under the table and paused. "Her plans changed?"

"Yes. She picked up a local assignment. Then she's leaving again." Luke emphasized the last part.

His mom tore down another box. "She deserves the truth. You've put it off long enough."

"After all these years, how was I to tell her? Email it? Call her up randomly? I said I'd tell her when I saw her next. She just never came home." He raked a hand through his hair before smoothing it.

"She's here now. You both need to clear the air. Consider it closure. For both of you."

"She may not be interested."

"She may not know she needs to hear what you have to say until you say it."

His mom had a point, Luke conceded. She always dispensed good advice, and he had carried Maren's secret long enough. But to lay his heart and soul bare? He refused to make their limited time together even more awkward. As for closure? He liked Shelby's smile and how her eyes twinkled. She had full lips that drew his attention and made him wonder if they tasted as sweet as when they'd been lovers. He was attracted to this older, wiser and more interesting woman. Whenever he was around her, his chest constricted and his breath held. "I'm sure we'll find the time to talk."

After all, they'd be in the air for hours.

"Good. It would make me happy for all of us to be friends again. Your dad and John, they'll eventually come around. You know why she's stayed away. She thought you cheated on her. Dumped her."

A few days after the funeral, Luke had told his mother what Maren had confessed. "I know it's my fault."

"You were young. Maren deceived you. It's wrong to speak ill of the dead, but she took advantage."

Luke hadn't realized Maren had been an Iago to his Othello until far too late. He believed Maren's lie, destroying his relationship with Shelby in the process. And then, fool he was, he'd turned to Maren afterward, as she'd been the sympathetic sounding board. She'd been safe. Once their marriage had begun to fail…well, Luke and his therapist had spent hours analyzing motivations, blind spots and action plans.

Those plans changed once she'd become sick. They'd changed again once Maren begged for his forgiveness and told him to go after Shelby.

"I did love Maren." At least in the beginning. Before he'd learned that everything was built on lies.

"Of course. But you were young. There are all kinds of love. Maren wasn't your soul mate. You can make the future whatever you want."

Luke wished. "Some people aren't like you and Dad, Mom. Soul mates are TV stuff. Shelby wanted to see the world and she has. Think about it. If she'd never left, would she have accomplished the things she has?"

As if tired of his justifications, his mom folded her arms. "Clear the air. It would be nice to have everyone together for Christmas for once."

"Fine." He'd always planned to tell Shelby the truth, even if she wouldn't fall into his arms afterward. "I'm seeing her later. Anna asked for another photography lesson."

"I love taking pictures." Hearing her name, Anna was back. "Can I go over to the inn and see Shelby? I know the way."

Luke's mom made a shooing motion. "Go ahead. Let me know if Laura made chocolate croissants. If so, bring me one."

As Anna darted off, Luke shifted. "I see what you're doing. I better go after her."

"Bring me one," his mom called to his backside.

Luke caught up to Anna as she knocked on the back door of the inn. Shelby's mom opened the kitchen door wide and a huge smile burst across her face. "Anna! Let me guess. You're here for a croissant."

"Yes!" Anna enthused. "And Grandma wants one, too."

"Oh, I saved one for her." Soon Shelby's mom had seated Anna at the kitchen table, a glass of hot cocoa and a flaky croissant the size of a woman's hand in front of her.

Footsteps sounded on the back stairs and Shelby

came into view. She was wearing a soft blouse tucked into a pair of cropped jeans that outlined her figure nicely, and he swallowed. No other woman had this immediate impact on him. Even when he'd called her "brace face"—he'd rightfully deserved the punch she'd landed on his bicep—Luke had thought her pretty both inside and out. Heck, he'd first kissed her when he'd been four. He'd declared her his girl-friend and planted a kiss on her lips. She'd smacked him then, too, come to think of it. Their parents, who'd seen the whole thing, had laughed. But in high school, that first kiss… The moment remained burned in his brain.

"Hi, Shelby!" Anna called.

"Hey." Shelby smoothed the surprise from her features. "Wasn't expecting to see you this early. Did you get the photos?"

"Dad did. May I have another lesson, please?" Anna took another bite.

"You got it." Shelby smiled at Anna, and Luke wished she'd look at him like that. Long ago she had.

"Can I talk to you?" Luke asked.

"Sure." Shelby snatched two croissants, wrapped them in a paper towel and pointed at the back door.

Luke led the way outside to their bench and a long ingrained habit made them sit in their usual spots.

She handed him one of the pastries. "Figured you'd like one, too."

"Thanks." He peeled off several light, flaky layers.

The buttery deliciousness melted against his tongue. "So good. Beats cereal."

They ate in silence for a moment before Luke decided to get to it. "The photos were great. You're a fabulous teacher. But you don't have to give Anna lessons. I'm sure you're busy."

"I know how to say no," Shelby snapped. Her lips thinned, daring him to contradict.

"I know you can, but..." That wasn't what he'd expected her to say. He stared, flummoxed.

"I enjoyed it. She's fun. You've done a good job raising her."

"She's made it easy. She's a good kid." Luke took another bite. Felt the awkwardness creep in. "I need to tell you something. About Maren."

Shelby quickly shook her head, making the blue ends of her ponytail swish. "No need. I've agreed to fly *Playgroup*. I've got four spreads riding on this, meaning completing the assignment for my editor is my top priority. Let's keep things professional. Keep the personal out. See? I can say no."

Her polite but firm smile sent the message loud and clear. A sense of frustration built. He wanted to tell her he hadn't cheated, that Maren had lied to each of them to drive them apart. Luke decided not to push. Not yet. He would find the right moment sometime in the next two weeks.

"Okay, balloon business only. We need to figure out when to practice. Last night my building permit came through, so I'll be busy overseeing contractors during the day."

"Congrats, the project's moving forward." Her smile became encouraging.

"I'm targeting a late October or early November opening. I'll know more in a week."

"I'm happy for you." Shelby put the last of the croissant in her mouth and thought for a moment. "Since Monday's out, what about tomorrow afternoon? With everyone busy at the festival, we should be able to lay *Playgroup* flat to check everything and perhaps even fly. Did the annual get done?"

The FAA required all hot-air balloons to undergo annual inspection, where technicians looked for wear, tear and damage. They tested the envelope fabric for strength, the temperature it could endure and porosity. They also checked the fuel system and various meters.

"Been in storage since Dad sent her off last October. We had to replace a few hoses and tanks, but nothing else. Basket was in great shape."

Her fingers flicked a loose crumb off her thigh. "I'll want to see the maintenance logs."

"Of course. They got checked, too. You know how meticulous our dads are in their record keeping."

"Military precision" Luke's mom had dubbed it. The way both men took care of their aircraft was more than a point of pride. Their lives, and those of anyone who flew with them, rested on the pilots' talents and the safety of the aircraft. He and Shelby had been raised not to cut corners.

"Perfect. *Playgroup* should be air-worthy. Do you have the flight manual?"

Like cars, boats and airplanes, each hot-air balloon had slightly different specifications depending on the manufacturer. He'd have to swipe the manual from his dad's desk, along with the storage-facility keys. "I'll bring it over tonight."

"Flying *Playgroup* has to be like riding a bike, right? While I've flown other balloons, it's been so long since I've taken her up." She gave him a nervous smile and he wished he could hug her.

"She'll forgive you." Luke rubbed his fingers together to remove some crumbs before using the napkin. He hoped Shelby would forgive him.

Shelby slid her hands under her thighs. A thin gold necklace circled her neck, met at the gap in her collarbone and then twisted together and fell as one strand before disappearing beneath her V-neck black silk camp blouse. "Let's hope she does."

"I'm sure she will. I'd forgive you."

"I'm not sure I'm guilty of anything." She tilted her chin slightly and stared at him. A wisp of loose hair slipped over her shoulder. He caught himself before he reached out and tucked it back behind her ear. Twelve years ago, he wouldn't have thought twice of touching her. By fall of his senior year, when his feelings had grown beyond friendship, he'd touched her often, whether a brief touch of her hand, or full contact, like when he'd wrestled her during that weekend game of football they'd played. She'd dared him to play on the other team, so he had. He hadn't let her score, and each time he'd tackled her, he'd held her extra tight. He could still picture her wicked expression as she'd rested, back to the grass, and how he'd lowered his mouth to kiss her, ignoring the get-a-room catcalls of their friends. From her faraway expression, he wondered if she was thinking of him, too.

"Shelby," Luke began, but the screen door banged, and Anna came racing out. Her feet pounded down the wooden steps.

"Dad! Mrs. Bien says if we don't go right now we'll miss the magic show."

"We can't have that." On cue, Shelby rose on scuffed white tennis shoes with a cheetah print star stitched onto the sides.

Luke masked his disappointment at Anna's interruption by smiling at his daughter. He couldn't help but catch Anna's excitement.

"Shelby, come, too," Anna invited. She stopped directly in front of her new friend.

"I…" Uncertain, Shelby looked at Luke.

"Shelby might have things to do," Luke said, trying to give Shelby an out without Anna being too disappointed. He didn't want Shelby to work with Anna out of a misguided sense of obligation, or assume he was foisting his daughter on her, or that she had to spend time with them. Although he wished she would spend as much time with him as possible.

"We could take more pictures. Please?" Anna's whole expression implored Shelby to cave, which, to Luke's surprise and joy, she did.

"Sure. It'll be fun. Tell you what, let me run inside, grab my camera and I'll join you. Be right back." The smile she directed at Anna tugged on Luke's heartstrings something fierce. "Don't leave without me," she called back as the screen door clattered.

"We won't." He meant every word. If he could, he wouldn't let her leave, either.

Anna skipped the few feet toward Luke. "See, Dad? She wanted to come. She's nice. I like Shelby."

I do, too, Luke thought. *I do, too.*

Shelby enjoyed the magic show. While no rabbits popped out of hats and no one got sawed in half, the magician dazzled with enough age-appropriate tricks in his half hour to keep both elementary-school kids and adults entertained.

Shelby took multiple pictures of the performance, concentrating some of her efforts on crowd shots. Kids and their parents laughed and clapped. Eyes and mouths opened wide in wonder. She captured the audience's joy as the magician hit his marks— reactions of oohs and aahs frozen forever.

When the show ended, the crowd dispersed and Shelby fell into step with Luke and Anna, as if they were a single unit. They strolled at a relaxed pace toward the railroad depot. Now a historical museum and Katy Trail pit stop, a Santa Fe train caboose sat out front on a short section of track. She and Luke had taken their homecoming pictures here, snippets of time preserved in photo albums.

"Anna loves trains," Luke said as Anna waited for her turn to climb aboard. "We did the Polar Express a few Christmases back in Ohio. There's something similar at Union Station, so I'll ask if she wants to go again. She might be outgrowing her train phase because she didn't want to set up her wooden train set. It hurts me more than her. I went all out buying things."

Luke had loved trains, Shelby remembered. There was a spot near the edge of town where they'd sit and count the coal cars as they rumbled by.

Anna's turn came and Luke lifted her onto the bottom step. She climbed up and waved off the back. "Look at me!" She acted as if she was pulling a train horn. "Toot! Toot!"

"Never gets old," Shelby said.

When Luke grinned, his smile consumed his face. Warmth spread through Shelby. When asked his best feature, she'd always say his smile, especially the one he reserved for her, like now.

To counteract her giddy overreaction, Shelby gave Luke a slight, purposeful shove. "Get up there. I'll take your picture."

"On my phone, too?" Luke passed over his iPhone and joined Anna on the back of the caboose. Shelby snapped away, laughing as he and Anna made various poses, some silly and some serious.

Shelby used her DSLR first, and then she let her camera hang by the strap as she pressed the button on his phone.

Then she heard someone call her name. "Shelby! What are you doing? Hand me that and get up there."

"Really, that's not necessary," Shelby protested as Mrs. James bustled over.

Mrs. James shooed her off. "There's no one waiting. Go."

Anna clapped her agreement. "Shelby, come stand by me."

Shelby set down her camera near Mrs. James and passed her Luke's cell phone. A tingle shot through Shelby as she accepted Luke's hand. His fingers laced through hers she climbed the step. She stood between him and Anna, and he slipped an easy arm behind her, as he'd done in the past. The casual gesture created a nerve-tingling zing.

Anna was all smiles. "Cheese!"

"You look so good together." Mrs. James gave Luke his phone and Shelby retrieved her camera. The weight of it didn't calm the aftershock of Luke's hand on her back.

Luke scrolled through the photos. "We do look great."

Shelby couldn't disagree. "I always forget how friendly Beaumont is. I'll upload these photos later today so you have them."

They walked toward Second Street. "What are your plans for the rest of the afternoon?" he asked casually, but Shelby heard serious interest.

"A shift at the duck pond. Maybe a bike ride. I didn't get enough of a run in this morning as I'd like."

As they navigated through the crowd, his hand brushed hers. "Would you like to join me and Anna tonight to watch the fireworks? If you're not going with your parents?"

A tiny thrill traveled from head to toe. More time with him and Anna? She liked the sound of that. But she hesitated. She was already too involved. "They didn't mention going."

"Watch with us!" Anna grabbed Shelby's hand. Her little fingers wrapped around Shelby's palm in a trusting grip that pierced Shelby's heart. "It'll be fun. Please." Anna drew out the word so it came out Plea-ease.

Shelby remained torn. Like her dad, Anna clearly had the gift of persuasion, and Anna continued to hold Shelby's hand. Her hand was a comfortable weight, a sensation as disconcerting as it was welcome. Shelby didn't regret not having children of her own, but she thought by this point she would have. She and Luke had planned on having, what…four? How young and foolish they'd been.

A group of teens laughing and paying little attention approached from the opposite direction. To protect her camera, Shelby let Anna's hand go. She sidestepped, but there wasn't enough room and a teen still bumped into her as he passed. Luke placed a hand on Shelby's lower back. A strong jolt shot through her, as if she'd seen a vision of her future—if she reached out and grabbed it. Her, Luke, Anna. One tight-knit little family. Maybe a child of their own.

Discombobulated, her toe caught a raised brick. She tripped but Luke caught her before she stumbled. "You okay?" he asked. Anna's worried face peered up at Shelby.

"Fine. Camera's safe." Shelby tried to make a joke of it. They stood by Gratiot House, one of Beaumont's oldest structures. Legend said it was haunted by a woman who'd died of cholera shortly after learning her husband had died while exploring the West. Heartbroken, she roamed several blocks of Main Street looking for him.

Must be the reason for the sudden chill, Shelby rationalized. The Woman in White, as locals called her, was no longer buried in the small graveyard at Third Street, as the bodies had been moved over a hundred years ago to a larger cemetery. However, people claimed they saw her as far down as First Street, near where she and her husband had once had their business, and she drew in the tourists for October's Haunted Beaumont tours.

"Shelby? You okay? You're pale," Luke said.

"Huh?" Shelby brushed off his concern. "Sorry. I spaced out. What'd you say?"

"I said if you'd like to join us, it'll give us a chance to talk about tomorrow's flight plans. And I'll get you the manual."

"How about I meet you at eight thirty? If I can join you, I will. If I not, I'll take it off your hands." She bit her lip.

"Sure. That'll work," he said, letting her off the hook.

She experienced a sliver of disappointment because he hadn't pressed, then chided herself for being silly. She was the one insisting on professionalism. Their parents' booths came into view, and Luke let Anna run ahead. "'Bye, Shelby!"

Shelby faced Luke. Took in the dip in his chin, the fullness of his expectant lips and the intensity of his gaze. Her breath hitched. "Until tonight."

"See you then." If they'd been dating, he'd kiss her goodbye. An impulse to touch her mouth to his grew. Did he kiss like she remembered? Would he make her toes tingle like before? As he shoved his hands in his front pockets and strolled toward the booth, Shelby went in the opposite direction.

The more time she spent with him, the more he slipped past her defenses and her mind screamed "run." She was attracted to the man he'd become, and longing made past sins easy to forget.

But she couldn't afford to get sidelined. Beaumont was like quicksand. The town could suck her in and kept her pleasantly unaware of the danger until she was unescapably in…too deep.

Luke planned to plant roots here. Once she had, too, but no longer. She should have him drop off the book. Put some serious distance between them before her wayward emotions overrode well-seasoned logic. She had assignments scheduled for the next six months and her career meant she was always on the road. They had no future. And he'd betrayed her in the past. Falling for him again would only lead to heartbreak.

Chapter Five

By eight, her resolve to text Luke and have him drop off the book fizzled. She'd worked the duck pond, taken more photos, spoken to her editor and grabbed a bike for a twenty-mile ride, ending in a second shower.

Excuses, Shelby knew. She was caving to her desire to see him. She stepped onto the wide front porch. An owl hooted. Down on the riverfront the band started playing and Shelby tapped her foot to the tune of a classic pop song.

She inhaled deeply, lifted her arms overhead and then circled her arms down to her sides in a slow, recharging motion. She could unwind in Beaumont, refill her soul. Unplug and be herself. However, if she stayed too long she would become like an overcharged battery. Expending the energy became essential to maintain longevity.

Restless, she slung her camera bag over her shoulder, walked to the booth and approached her mom. "Where does Luke live?"

If her mom found the question odd, she answered without comment. "In the apartment over the art gallery. Side door."

Shelby glanced at her watch. If she hurried, she could catch him before he left to meet her at the inn. Shelby crossed the street. A narrow concrete sidewalk ran between the art-gallery building and its neighbor, and Shelby slipped into the four-foot gap and rang the doorbell.

Luke opened the door. "Hey, Shelby."

Suddenly a preemptive strike didn't seem so smart. She shifted her weight. "I figured I'd swing by and grab the manual. Save you the trip. This way I don't intrude on your evening."

Luke frowned. "You aren't intruding. The book's upstairs. Come on up."

See Luke's place? "I'm good here."

Bare feet pounded down the stairs and Anna appeared around Luke's legs. She had on pajamas and her hair dripped a few droplets on her shoulders. "Shelby! You're here! I knew you'd come."

Luke opened the door wider. While he didn't call Shelby a "chicken" like he'd done when they were kids, she heard it, anyway. Saw what he was holding back in the curl of his lips and the speculative arch of his left eyebrow.

It was silly to refuse. She stepped past him, followed Anna up the narrow stairs set between brick walls and entered the apartment, highly aware of Luke behind her. They reached the landing, and curiosity won. Whoever redesigned the space had retained the historical charm, leaving the brick exterior walls bare and the golden hardwood floors uncovered. The apartment had ten-foot ceilings, and tall windows ran the entire wall overlooking Main. The open concept also contained modern features like exposed ductwork, stainless-steel appliances and granite countertops.

A wooden closet door hosted Anna's pictures, which were taped in neat rows. Luke had printed two of Anna's photos and taped them onto a kitchen cabinet. Barbie dolls rested haphazardly on an oversize braided area rug, and a box of crayons and coloring books sat on the coffee table. The decor spoke of one thing: home. The room's warmth drew Shelby like an electromagnet. The deep leather couch was designed to sit with a cup of coffee and watch… She smiled. Magical ponies danced on the 65-inch TV.

Luke pointed to the kitchen counter. "The manual is there. Make yourself comfortable. I'm helping Anna dry her hair. We'll be right out."

"Don't leave, Shelby! I want you to see my room!" Anna disappeared down a hall with Luke hard on her heels.

Not wanting to disappoint Anna—she'd go with
that excuse—Shelby set down her camera bag and
slid onto a counter stool. On the big screen, the ponies sang about the joy of being friends. She opened
the manual and skimmed several pertinent parts.
She'd read more thoroughly later; her concentration
was shot. The contrast between her and Luke's apart-
ments was stark. He had a home; she had a place to
store clothes. Anna came racing down the hallway,
her dry hair billowing.

"Come on!" Anna grabbed Shelby's hand and
tugged.

"Okay. Okay." Shelby laughed and allowed Anna
to pull her along. Anna's bedroom was the first door
down the hall, for which Shelby was grateful. She
wondered what Luke's bedroom looked like, but better to avoid temptation. Did he have a photo of Maren
on his bedside table?

She shoved aside the small jealous flare. Despite
how things ended, she never would have wished for
Luke to lose Maren, or Anna her mother. Shelby
would never wish him—or Maren—ill for finding
each other. Maybe recognizing that fact was the first
step to healing.

Shelby gave her full attention to Anna's show-
and-tell. She oohed and aahed over the items Anna
dragged out. She offered genuine responses, which
required expert concentration. Not because it was
hard to follow a kindergartner who talked rapid-fire,
but rather because Luke lounged in the doorway,

making Shelby hyperaware. Seeing him with his daughter tugged her heartstrings. Made her desire things she couldn't have.

Knowing he was studying her with his hooded gaze, Shelby kept her back to him. If she caught his eye, she might reveal too much. He might see the truth of what she kept hidden deep inside—that for all her globetrotting, she was still a woman who wanted to dive in. Be head over heels in love with her soul mate and live happily-ever-after with him and their children.

She admired Anna's collection of music boxes, telling Anna about her Swiss chalet until Luke gruffly cleared his throat. "I know you two are having a blast, but it's almost fireworks time."

Shelby readied to make her excuses. Then Anna slipped her hand into Shelby's and she couldn't do it. Throat dry, Shelby followed Luke into the living room. She'd already stowed the manual into her camera bag, and she slung the bag over her shoulder. "Shall we?"

"I thought we'd watch on our rooftop," Luke said. "I promise the view's worth it. And we can bring snacks and adult beverages."

He'd known she planned to bow out, which was probably why Anna was in pajamas. He'd expected her to come here preemptively and knew she wouldn't be able to resist once she did.

"Can we eat the sprinkle cookies we got from Mrs. James?" Anna asked.

"Of course," Luke said. He caught her gaze and winked. "Shelby loves cookies."

"We got six. Dad said I could eat yours if you had to cancel." Anna grabbed Shelby's hand and swung her arm, which kept Shelby from facing Luke while she gathered her composure. How infuriating that he could still read her.

When she turned, he raised both eyebrows in confirmation. "You'll love the rooftop. Anna can show you the way. She can't go up there unless she's with an adult and you count."

Shelby tilted her head. Tried for levity. "Last time I checked."

"Which is why I'll bring some wine." When he winked, something inside her jumped.

"This way." Anna pulled eagerly on Shelby's arm.

Shelby held position and gave Anna the expression mothers around the world used. "Let's ask if your dad needs help."

"Dad, do you need help?" Anna asked dutifully.

Luke stood in the kitchen. "I got it. Go on up."

Anna raced to the end of the hall. Shelby quickly glanced into Luke's bedroom and saw a plaid bedspread. Anna pointed at the dead bolt. "You have to unlock."

"I can do that." Shelby turned the shoulder-height dead bolt and flipped the light switch, revealing indoor fire stairs. At the top, she opened another door. Solar lights set in planters illuminated a pathway and an area of the roof closest to the water.

"That one." Anna pointed and Shelby flipped another switch, making a series of overhead string lights glow. Hundreds of tiny bulbs lit up a large section of rooftop, creating a magical effect. In the center, two outdoor sectional love seats and one chair surrounded an oversize square fire pit. Luke arrived, juggling a tray filled with napkins, a juice box for Anna, a plate of sprinkle cookies, two plastic stemless wineglasses and a bottle of Riesling with a convenient screw cap. Shelby took the tray and put it on the table, ignoring the zing of their fingers touching.

Propane flames created a soft glow. Shelby chose the chair. Watched as Luke passed Anna a cookie and juice. He opened the wine and poured her a glass, which she set on the table so that he could pass her a cookie. He served himself and settled onto the love seat to her left.

"Sprinkles are my favorite," Anna announced from the other love seat. She broke her cookie in half.

"We'll turn off the lights when the fireworks begin. We may have to stand, but we'll see them perfectly."

"It's nice up here." Besides the lights, pots held flowers and herbs that were starting to go dormant. In another corner was a hammock, and in another, a metal bistro table with two matching chairs.

"Thanks. The decking was here, but I did the rest. It's farmland across the river so you can really see the stars."

He opened a plastic cubicle that served as an end

table and removed fuzzy throws similar to those at the inn. He passed blankets to Anna and Shelby. Anna snuggled under hers and began playing on her handheld game.

Not cold, Shelby set the throw on the opposite cushion. She lifted the camera with its attached 70-200 mm lens. A tripod wasn't worth returning for; she wouldn't be making long exposure shots that required the camera to be propped. She adjusted the ISO, aperture and shutter speed, then rose and walked to the brick railing surrounding the perimeter. She could clearly see the bandstand and hear the lead singer announce the final song. "I talked to my sister. What time shall we go?"

Shelby returned to the sofa and took a sip of the crisp white wine. "Three? So we get into the air by four? Does that work?"

"Should. The booths close at five. Anna will hang out with Riley." Shelby remembered Luke's teenage niece. "I told Lisa we'd call once we pulled out the envelope and straightened the lines. She and Carl can be there within fifteen minutes to help us launch."

As a cheer erupted from the riverfront crowd, Shelby leaned back against comfortable cushions as a mellow, relaxing mood overtook her. "I could get used to this. My building has a rooftop but it's party central. Too crowded."

"I agree I'm spoiled. You like Seattle?"

Shelby spun the glass slowly and watched the liquid catch the ambient light. "I guess. I'm never there.

These last four months I've been crisscrossing the United States. Colorado was white-water rafting and mountain climbing. Arizona was hiking the Grand Canyon. I drove in from Iowa."

Luke made a face. "Iowa's flat and boring."

"Not as much as you think. Northeast Iowa has steep hills and valleys reminding me of the Ozarks. I photographed a scenic railroad. There's paddle boarding on Gray's Lake. Not all of our readers are fitness buffs so we feature all levels of outdoor adventures. It's one reason the magazine continues to grow."

"You love what you do."

Pride and pleasure that he'd noticed made her nod. "I do. Mark Twain said, 'Travel is fatal to prejudice, bigotry and narrow-mindedness, and many of our people need it sorely on these accounts.'"

"That's a mouthful."

She sipped more wine, her inner English-minor geek emerging. "It is, but it stuck with me. There's more." She paused. Remembered. "He also said 'Broad, wholesome, charitable views of men and things cannot be acquired by vegetating in one little corner of the earth all one's lifetime.' I made that last part my personal philosophy. When I'm on assignment, I'm bringing adventure to my readers. If they can't get to the world, I bring the world to them."

"Didn't Twain settle down in Connecticut? Like built a house in Hartford?"

Shelby understood Luke's point. "Twain's not say-

ing there's something wrong with roots. Just vegetating all of one's lifetime in one place and never
experiencing things. Having a home base is fine."

Although Seattle was more of a jumping-off point
than a home. A whizzing sound whistled through the
air and Shelby glanced up. Anna put down her game.
"They're starting!"

Luke flipped a switch, plunging the rooftop into
darkness minus the few path lights and the fire.
Shelby grabbed her camera, but she didn't need to
stand. Her vantage point offered the perfect view of
the fireworks bursting overhead. She snapped about
forty pictures before setting the camera aside so she
could enjoy subsequent bursts with the naked eye.
She caught Luke's stare and automatically wiped her
lips for crumbs. "What?"

"Nothing. Just glad you're here." The darkened
rooftop hid her blush, and Shelby tipped her face upward. Several red-chrysanthemum fireworks burst,
forming a flowerlike pattern. White waterfalls followed.

She held her breath as dragon's eggs crackled in
the night sky, remembering the last time they'd seen
fireworks, and the last time they'd seen each other.
On New Year's, when the world had been full of
promise and love.

She'd seen and photographed dozens of fireworks
shows since. Over on her love seat, Anna clapped
and oohed, so Shelby made a quick adjustment to her

camera, and captured the bursts of light reflected on Anna's excited face.

Shelby twisted the lens again, checked the settings and pressed her finger down for continuous shots as the finale began.

Then the booming stilled, and like a one-second delay on live television, anticipatory silence reigned. Smoke drifted east, carried on a gentle breeze away from Beaumont. Then the riverfront crowd cheered again. Covered with the blanket, Anna closed her eyes and seconds later let out a soft snore. Shelby gazed at the sky. Luke hadn't been kidding about the stars. She aimed her lens and surveyed before lowering the camera.

"You're staring." She sucked in a breath. Heightened tension vibrated like a plucked guitar string.

His lashes flickered, his expression intense and guilt-free. "I was. Besides taking pictures for the yearbook, I've never seen you work. You're totally into it. I can see why you're so good."

His compliment made her insides gooey. "It's a nerdy vocation."

"Don't sell yourself short. The way you can adjust things and automatically know the right settings is amazing. Remember how you tried to teach me? Epic fail. Those people who say anyone can do it are fools."

"It's a lot of trial and error. It took a long time to get it right. Some of my college classes were really rough. You put your images up there and they aren't as good as your classmates'. It's quite humbling."

She sighed. "Winning a contest wasn't a free pass. My biggest reality check was learning that photography is not a glamourous vocation. Most of the time it's a lot of sitting out in the rain and other elements and waiting forever for the perfect shot. It's a lifestyle where I buy extra T-shirts so I have clean clothes. A White House photographer I know says he has at least a hundred unwashed shirts in his apartment because he's never home to do laundry. It's simply easier to open a new shirt each day."

Luke reached for another cookie. "I had no idea."

"I've figured some tricks along the way. When stateside, I ship clothes home in priority flat-rate boxes so I have room in my suitcase for new stuff. I get home and drop off one suitcase and grab another already packed. It's nonstop travel, but also a lot of waiting around. But the scenery is incredible. Just never permanent."

Maybe drinking wine had loosened her tongue, as she kept talking. Then again Luke had always been the world's best listener. "In Iowa, I photographed a proposal. Actually, it was a hot-air-balloon landing. The proposal was a bonus. I gave chase because it was fun. Not work, but fun. The camera changes how you see the world, so it's nice to sit back sometimes and rediscover why I love what I do."

She sipped from the wineglass. "It's one reason why I like teaching Anna."

Shelby gestured to Luke's daughter, who was sleeping with her mouth open. "To her it's just pictures. She has raw, innocent joy. Me? My favorite thing is my job."

"What about running? Cycling?"

"Those keep me in shape because the job is physical." Shelby stretched her legs. Her life sounded mundane. "I'm not home to cook. I'm hardly in town to see friends on a constant basis."

Anna sat up with a start. "Dad, I need to go potty."

"You can go by yourself," Luke said. "Turn the lights on."

Anna darted off the couch, switched on the overhead lights and raced down the stairs.

Luke watched her go. Exhaled. "It's good we've come home. In Cincinnati, I felt like I was going through the motions. I worked long hours. Even before Maren died, I realized I'd lost sight of what was important to me. I asked myself, was I on the partnership treadmill because it was expected or because I loved the rush? I learned work doesn't keep one warm at night or make me satisfied."

"I love to take pictures," Shelby defended, as he'd hit the nail on the head and that rankled slightly. "It's not just work. These spreads matter. It's a huge accomplishment to be the first female featured."

"And I'm thrilled for you. But what then? What's next? Like, don't photographers sometimes give themselves challenges for the fun of it? Say photographing all blue things one day or red the next?"

He'd voiced one of her greatest fears—that she'd stop enjoying her craft. "Where'd you hear that? You didn't take Mrs. Benedict's photojournalism class."

"I took an intro-to-photography class for my college art credit."

Her heart gave a skip. "Really?"

"Don't look so surprised. I thought it might help me understand what photography meant to you. Maybe give us something to talk about. But I never saw you again."

"You were dating Maren, anyway. But let's not talk about that and ruin the night."

"Sorry. I didn't mean to bring up the past." He began to put the napkins and juice box onto the tray.

Standing, she retrieved the half-full bottle of wine and her camera bag. "It's late. We have a big day tomorrow and I'm sure it's past Anna's bedtime. She fell asleep."

"She enjoyed you being here."

"I liked it, too." Far too much. Sitting by the fire, the night had softened her. She'd imagined another life, one spent sitting on a couch with Luke, his arm around her, tracing the Big Dipper and finding Orion like they'd done so many times before. "Can I carry anything else?"

"I got it." He turned off the fire pit, picked up the tray. When they reached the second floor, Anna stepped out of the bathroom.

"Go dry your hands," Luke instructed as he passed

by, and Anna darted back into the bathroom to comply. He grinned. "Kids."

Shelby set the wine bottle on a kitchen counter. Barefoot, Anna padded into the living room still wearing her pink pajama top and matching leggings. "I brushed my teeth, too."

"Good job. Tell Shelby good-night. You can read for a while and then I'll check on you."

"Okay." Anna threw her arms around Shelby's thighs and squeezed tight. "Good night, Shelby. I love you."

The unexpected hug and subsequent declaration floored Shelby, but Anna didn't seem to require any response. Instead, she gave her dad a kiss and flew back down the hallway to her room. "Is that normal?"

"Very," Luke reassured her.

Shaken by Anna's declaration, Shelby adjusted the camera bag. "I don't want to crush her spirit or anything. I'm leaving. I don't want her to become too attached."

In an act of comfort, Luke put his hand lightly on Shelby's forearm. His fingers fused to her skin. "She'll be fine. She understands people don't all live in Beaumont. We visited her grandparents in Florida over Labor Day weekend."

"Good." Shelby exhaled a long breath and dropped her arm away from his magnetic touch. The last person she would ever want to crush would be Anna. "I should go."

Sensing the shift, Luke said, "I'll walk you out."

He followed her down to the sidewalk. He stood in the doorway, not too close but not too far away. If he leaned forward, his mouth would come closer, and it frightened her how she wanted his kiss. "Thanks for watching with us," Luke said.

She bit her lip. *Focus on flying. Not the texture of Luke's mouth or how the exterior light created sexy shadows, defining his cheekbones.* "Tomorrow. Meet you here?"

"That'll work."

An imperceptible pause occurred as time dropped away, as if they'd never separated these past twelve years. She recognized his desire. Knew he longed for a kiss, as she did. Fireworks and Luke. She wanted more nights like this.

Wanted him.

She couldn't risk the hopeful emotions entering the equation. She would be leaving in two weeks. She needed to go now, before he saw through her and realized how cowardly she was.

"Good night, Luke. See you tomorrow."

His voice carried on the light wind. "Good night, Shelby. Sleep well."

Chapter Six

Sunday started off as one of those days. Her dreams the night before hadn't helped. She'd been slow dancing with Luke. Then she'd been in the woods, unable to find him. She'd jolted awake, breathing heavily.

On the morning run to clear her head, she'd broken her shoelace. At breakfast, she'd spilled her coffee, which necessitated a change of clothes and mopping up the mess.

After that inauspicious start, the day calmed down. She uploaded and sorted pictures, emailing Luke that Anna's new images were ready. She sent two dozen photos to her editor a day early. She helped her mother with some routine cleaning. She took a few hours to read a novel, Boba sleeping in her lap. As the appointed hour of meeting Luke drew nearer, she reviewed the manual and promptly started yawning.

With her watch over on the dresser and being too lazy to go over and grab it, she set the timer on her phone for fifteen minutes and closed her eyes. She woke up when her phone began to shrill.

"Are you coming?" Luke asked when she answered.

Shelby bolted upright and glanced at the wall clock. Three fifteen. She stared at her phone. The timer read 15:00. Either she'd slept through the timer hitting zero or it hadn't worked. "On my way."

Five minutes later, camera bag and manual in hand, she met Luke at the side door. His long-sleeve polo tucked into jeans made him appear totally put-together; she was rumpled in a wrinkled shirt that was hanging loose. "My alarm didn't go off."

"Happens to the best of us. You always were on time so I figured I best call."

"Glad you did or I would have kept napping." Which was embarrassing. At least she'd checked the weather conditions. "Let's launch from the town race field. It's dry and wind's westward, so we won't fly over the festival."

A diesel dually, crew cab pickup waited behind his building and Shelby slid onto the leather passenger seat. "Yours?"

"Yeah, on two-year lease. Comes in handy with hauling things for the renovations."

Once at the storage unit, Luke backed the truck to the garage door, jumped out and hitched up the trailer. Shelby took some quick pictures before they drove to the town park, where Luke backed the trailer against the curb. Shelby stood beside him as he opened the double doors and pulled out the storage bag containing the envelope. Leaving the basket in the trailer, Luke dragged the bag onto the grass and he and Shelby withdrew the contents.

And stared at the mess before them. All the ropes and lines were tangled.

"Crap," Luke said. A stricken look on his face, he raked his hand through his hair. "I don't believe this. I had no idea. Sorry."

Shelby's decision came instantaneously. She took a step back and shook her head, her ponytail swishing. "Call your sister. Tell her we don't need her. We're not flying today."

Luke moved the storage bag aside and frowned. "It'll take us some time to straighten the lines but there's plenty of daylight left."

She hadn't made herself clear. "No. That's three strikes. We'll untangle the lines but that's it."

"Got it." Without hesitation, Luke dug in his pocket for his phone. Three strikes was a superstitious rule many pilots had about flying: if three things went wrong before takeoff and if you could still abort the flight, you did.

"So what were they?" Luke asked.

Shelby squatted low and lifted one of the ropes. "Shoelace broke, spilled my coffee, you had to wake me up and now this. I guess that's four strikes. Five if you count I didn't sleep well." Shelby studied the tangles, which appeared like a huge ball of knotted fishing lines. "We have our work cut out for us. Always an adventure, right?"

"Well, at least it's solid proof our dads took her straight for her annual after last year's race and she's not been out since."

Shelby moved the lines and sighed. "The technicians certainly shoved her back in there. Let's get started. I'll take this end."

She sat on the soft grass and Luke dropped next to her, close enough that his aftershave mixed with the gentle breeze. She ignored the tingle of being mere inches apart and focused on working methodically, lifting ropes and following them through the knot. "Okay, this one goes under here," Shelby said, and Luke threaded the line back.

Slowly the tangle loosened and the lines straightened. Occasionally, their hands would touch and their thighs would brush, and a little flutter of something Shelby refused to acknowledge prickled her skin. Luke had sex appeal in spades and a kindhearted, decent soul.

Though their work was tedious, the temperature and day remained goldilocks-perfect, and as they unraveled the lines, the conversation between them grew easier. They stayed on safe topics, such as what had happened to people they knew from high school. Matt Clark had become a Wall Street banker. The town bookstore had hosted a huge event when Mimi Swearingen published her first novel.

They were down to the last few knots when Luke took a deep breath that made Shelby instinctively tense. He blurted out, "Maren told me you hated the fact we'd made love and you no longer wanted to be with me. I know now what she said was all a lie."

Shelby's hand froze. The revelation had come out of the blue. "What? Repeat that."

Luke dropped the line and faced her. "A week before she died, Maren wanted to clear her conscience. She felt she tricked me into loving her and wanted me to forgive her. I thought maybe the pain meds were making go her out of her mind, but that day she was lucid. You'd given her my address. For England."

Shelby tried to process what he was saying. "Everyone in town had your email so they could write you while you were gone."

"She told me you felt our relationship was a mistake. That you'd met someone else and didn't want to hurt me. It's why I pulled back."

Stunned, Shelby dropped her hands into her lap. "I told you I loved you every time I wrote. At least at first."

She paused. In the beginning of his absence, she'd written "I love you" on every piece of correspondence, complete with hearts and *XOXOXO*. She'd mailed a card a day. But then as Luke's letters and emails had become shorter, she'd dropped the hearts, dropped the *X*'s and *O*'s, sent a card a week, then maybe every two weeks, and emailed about the weather. Her cat. Things of no consequence that didn't require emotions.

Luke picked at the grass, then brushed it off his jeans. "She said you were being nice because you didn't want to send me a Dear John letter or break up via email. She said you did it so it didn't strain our parents' friendship."

Shelby closed her eyes and let the blackness come. Opened her eyes to see the anguished expression on Luke's face. "She convinced me you'd met someone in London, which is why you were short with me. Why you stopped telling me you loved me. So I did the same as not to pressure you."

"I figured we'd clear the air when I got home, but you were in Wyoming. Then you chose to go to college in Seattle and went straight there. Maren said…" Luke raked a hand through his hair and then swiped his hand through the grass. "I didn't want to attend Mizzou without you. Especially after our fight."

The verbal weapons they'd thrown at each other. Shelby shuddered.

"She was my shoulder to cry on. And Cincinnati seemed far enough away from the memories. In retrospect, following her was dumb decision. My pride getting in the way."

"She told me you were dating. That you'd cheated on me, with her."

"I know. She told me you were cheating, too. I didn't cheat. And for the record, Maren and I didn't even date until our junior year of college, after I took her to a frat event. We fell into it because everyone seemed to be a couple, and well, she'd always been there. I know I'm pathetic. I let her hang around and because of that she kept hoping she'd be the one. Eventually I let her since she'd always had my back." He paused, his eyes pleading. "How could I date anyone else after you? I couldn't. Not until I realized we were truly done several years later after I never saw you again."

"I don't know whether to laugh or cry." Overwhelmed with turbulent emotions, Shelby tried not to tremble. She felt as if a rug had been yanked out from underneath her and she'd fallen on her back. She peered up at the sky, which remained a placid blue.

Luke went to touch her hand and then checked the movement. "I deserve every bit of your condemnation and hate. I hate myself. I was young and stupid, but it's no excuse for what I did. For what I said to you."

It took every ounce of her willpower not to scream in frustration. She would never have imagined this—although in hindsight, perhaps the clues were there.

"People say I broke your heart, not that you broke mine. Then again, I wasn't here to defend myself, not that it's anyone's business."

Luke winced. "I'm sorry for that. Losing you broke my heart. I believed you'd found someone else. I wasn't good enough. It did a number on me."

Shelby stood. Prayer hands covered her nose and mouth. Her chest heaved as the enormity of Luke's revelation and the depth of Maren's trickery hit her. She paced, whirled and paced again.

"Shelby, are you okay?" Luke rose but gave her space.

"No. I'm trying not to curse the dead." She hiccupped out her next words. "I loved you. I was so happy when we were together." She grabbed a water bottle and took a long drink. Drew a deep breath. "All I heard from Maren was how I wasn't sophisticated enough to keep your interest, especially with all those English girls around. Then when I was in Wyoming, she'd email me all the things the two of you were doing. I called you and she answered."

"She picked up my phone. And I'll never forgive myself for what happened next."

She'd accused him of cheating on her with Maren. He'd denied it—why would Maren lie? Then Luke had accused her of cheating on him. They'd fought long-distance with the immaturity of eighteen-year-olds who didn't trust their love, each broken by the full intensity of believing they'd been wronged.

When the call disconnected, it was the last time they'd spoken…until running into each other in the cookie store.

Shelby shook with rage, her whole body livid with loss and grief. Luke approached, but she held up her hands to keep him back. He stilled. "I believe you. How could I not see what a toxic person she was? Was I so desperate and lonely that I needed her friendship?"

"I asked myself the same questions, but much later after I married her. We had issues, ones that got worse over time. We were discussing getting divorced before she got sick. I couldn't leave her then, especially as we had Anna. I had no idea how deep her lies went until she begged me to forgive her."

Shelby's hands flew into her hair and for a moment she gripped her ponytail and tugged hard, the pain welcome. His revelations had shredded the whole foundation of who she was, what she'd believed. "This is a lot to take in."

"I know. I'm sorry I turned to her after I thought you didn't love me. When I learned the truth, she was sick, you were traveling all over the world and my whole life had been upended. Not only did I find out what she'd done, but I also had to make Anna a priority. It's not about me anymore."

"You aren't the victim here," Shelby snapped.

Luke's tone gentled. "No, we both are. I've simply had more time to come to terms with it. You meant the world to me. I loved you. I hurt you. I should have come after you that summer. Refused to let you push me away. Fought for us. Ever since I learned the truth two years ago, I've wanted to tell you I'm sorry, make amends. But I couldn't just call you out of the blue and say 'hey, Maren lied.' It had to be said in person."

Shelby credited him for that wisdom. She would have hung up. Blocked his number. Returned any letters unopened.

"I'm the reason you don't come home and visit your parents more."

"I would never give you that power," Shelby growled, even though in a sense she had done that by staying on the road as long as she did. She regrouped. Calmed. "I'm glad you told me. It helps somewhat."

"I've had two years of counseling to help me deal with the shock. Even more before that when I realized marrying Maren was a mistake."

Shelby clung tight to one truth. Her lips twisted wistfully. "The fact remains that we were young. We fell apart at the first external pressure we faced. I'm a believer that fate takes us where we are supposed to be. You know, way leads on to way. You wouldn't have Anna otherwise."

"She's one good thing that came out of this. Did you know Maren was in remission when they moved to Beaumont? They came to be closer to a specialist. She only told me our senior year of college because the signs didn't look good. All she wanted was a family. A child."

And Luke was an honorable man, Shelby knew. Maren's illness explained her destructive and desperate behavior. It didn't excuse it, but it allowed Shelby to find empathy.

Luke wrung his hand before swiping back his hair. "Therapy helped me realize I'm allowed to be happy again. I'm allowed to find and have the deep, all-encompassing love I see in our parents."

Shelby's heart broke, but she refused to cry for what might have been. She shook her head. "But not with me. Our lives are too different. I'm all over the world and you have Anna. Despite Maren's lies, perhaps she was right to break us up. You would have felt guilty tying me to Beaumont, so you'd have moved to Seattle and in turn hated living in a small apartment waiting for me to come home only to leave again. We'd have been miserable."

Speaking the words aloud solidified them. Luke didn't answer, and Shelby moved to take his hands in hers. Felt the warmth as he gripped her tight. Sensed his strength, and recognized how much he'd gone through to put himself mentally aright.

"Thank you. Telling me this has helped me, especially knowing you didn't break my heart on purpose. I'll never again have to wonder if I did something wrong or if I wasn't good enough. You and me, we can be friends. Not as we were, but something. And eventually you'll find someone who lives here and who makes you happy, and she'll be that forever love where you sit on the front porch in rocking chairs when you're old. And I'll be happy for you instead of insanely jealous."

But with their hands fused together, she knew that deep down she'd always be jealous of anyone who dated Luke. She'd always want him to pick her over everyone else. But this time, unlike when they were in high school and she thought he'd rejected her, this time they were adults with jobs, lives and responsibilities. They now had miles between them, not misunderstandings. This time saying no and leaving was her choice. Being with Luke meant home and hearth, and Shelby was suitcase and global adventure, her career achievements within reach.

"You do have to forgive her," she urged Luke. "She was wrong. But she loved you and gave you Anna. And Anna is so wonderful, so lovable." Shelby would miss her when she left. She'd miss Luke, too.

"I know. But seeing you standing in Auntie Jayne's floored me. What might have been? We loved each other so much."

Her heart fluttered, but she ignored the hope trying to bloom. "It doesn't matter. The past is done and gone. We move forward. Fly *Playgroup*. Even if not today. Let's get the lines straightened, pack her up and try again later this week."

"Sounds like a good idea," Luke agreed. "I'd like that."

He didn't appear totally happy, but Shelby wasn't about to let them wallow in the past. After letting go of Luke's hands, she checked the weather app on her phone. "How about flying on Tuesday? Will that work? I know it's a weekday."

"I'll check with Carl and Lisa. They are usually pretty flexible since Lisa works with Mom, and Carl works from home. Can you meet me at Caldwell's? Say around two thirty? I'd like to show you what I'm doing. Then we can go."

"Sure. See, we're already on our way to being friends." Shelby settled down next to the ropes again, and soon her leg pressed against his. Their hands touched as they exchanged rope pieces. But she ignored the butterflies flitting in her stomach. Pushed away the delicious scent of his aftershave. Her fingers itched to run over his rock-hard, denim-covered thigh, but that's not what friends did. She stood and moved to another line.

Once they finished untangling, they laid out the fabric envelope. *Playgroup* was a 90, which meant 90,000 cubic feet, bigger than a 77—the more common size in Missouri and most eastern states. When Shelby and Luke's dads had decided to purchase their own balloon, they'd chosen one that could easily lift a basket with a pilot, minister and a wedding couple.

Satisfied everything looked good, they repacked

the components, put the envelope in the bag, gave the basket a quick inspection and returned everything to the trailer. "Shall we stop for dinner? We're not due back for a bit," he said.

She should go home. But even though any romantic relationship with Luke could never be possible, she didn't want the day to end. Why not explore this new friendship? He'd been one of the most important people in her life; surely, they could forge a new path. Even if it meant ignoring the spark of longing she felt. "Sure."

They returned the trailer to the storage unit, but instead of heading toward Main Street, Luke drove to the next town over, to Angel's Diner, one of their old haunts. From the exterior, Angel's looked like a dive. However, it served the best Mexican food in the county. Proof that what was on the inside was what really mattered.

Their old favorite booth was available, and Shelby slid onto familiar brown wood. Across the table, Luke sat in the same spot he'd occupied many years before. Along with two menus, the waitress brought a basket of tortilla chips and a dish of *pico de gallo*. She left after taking their order of one beer and one margarita.

"I'm guessing you still love queso and guac?" Luke asked.

She appreciated his attempt to return things to

normal. "Absolutely. I hope it's as good as I remember. Have you been back much?"

"Not since we were here last. My parents eat at the new place in town."

Pleased that it remained "their place," Shelby assessed the decent-size dinner crowd. "How many times did we come here?"

"Seemed all the time once I got my license. Five dollars' worth of tacos and water."

Shelby laughed. "Yeah. You paid for gas and tacos and I bought the queso."

"A fair deal," Luke acknowledged. "And we ate at least five baskets of chips."

And they were already halfway through the first basket. Shelby dug out a few broken fragments and dipped them into the *pico de gallo*.

Luke began to read the menu. "Tonight I'm ordering something besides tacos. And water."

They shared a secret smile when the waitress arrived with two tall plastic cups of water and additional chips. As Shelby lifted the first chip from the new basket to her mouth, she started laughing, uncaring when people nearby stared.

In response, Luke deliberately put another chip in his mouth. She didn't even have to explain to Luke what she found funny. He understood the irony— now that they could afford to eat anywhere, they were in their old stomping grounds scarfing down chips.

"I'm getting the enchiladas. And a taco for old time's sake. I'll run at least five miles tomorrow to make up for it."

"I'm an early riser now. I could join you." Luke made the casual offer at the same time the waitress set down a bowl of warm, creamy queso cheese and a bowl of thick, chunky guacamole. Exercising with Luke could be interesting. They used to run together in high school. Elbows on the table, she held her hands up, a chip in her left fingers. "Maybe."

He flattened his palms on the table. "A *maybe*? That's it?"

"Yeah. Because you'd be tempted to race me, and I'm not hurting the renewal of our friendship by kicking your butt and humiliating you."

He leaned forward and his lips puckered as he issued the challenge. "You think you can win?"

She scoffed, her tone light but serious. "I know I can."

Admittedly, he was no slacker in the fitness department. He had muscles in all the right places. Their adult beverages thankfully arrived as a welcome diversion.

"To fresh starts." Luke's eyes twinkled as Shelby brought her margarita to his beer mug in a satisfying clink.

She took a sip. "Ooh. This is good. If I'd come here at twenty-one, it would have been hangover city."

And with that, she began to tell Luke about her

adventures. He laughed at the right places. Didn't douse her with concern at others. He asked questions that led her down new, interesting tangents.

"Everest was one of my favorites," she told him. "There's something so humbling about standing at the bottom. Everyone is there for a common purpose, to summit and survive. You learn what really matters. You realize how insignificant a lot of things really are."

"Would you go back?"

She shook her head. "No. I realized Everest is not something I must conquer."

She sipped the last of her margarita, the ice remnants rattling in the glass. He'd listened so well during dinner, deliberately letting her dominate the conversation. She ate a forkful of the honey-drizzled, powdered-sugar-covered sopaipilla. The deep-fried pastry was delicious. "You know, you could have jumped in. I don't remember you holding back before."

Relaxed, he leaned back. "I liked hearing the stories firsthand. I've missed this. Talking with you. Sharing things."

"Me, too," she admitted, even though it scared her how in sync they remained. "But you told me so little about you."

He shrugged. "Not much to tell. Work, cancer, kid."

She refused to allow melancholy to invade. "Those are adventures enough." She reached her hand across the table and covered his. Her palm fused to the back of his hand until he flipped his arm and wrapped his fingers through hers. She enjoyed the sensation. "I have global texting. I'll send you pictures of everything from here forward."

His thumb made a circle inside her hand. "I'd like that. Your friendship was one of the most important of my life. I don't want to lose touch again."

"We won't," Shelby promised, although she couldn't be certain. She wanted to believe they could be friends. Do more things like tonight whenever she visited. However, as she reached for the bill, her hand missed his touch. She noted how easily the longing returned.

To keep the mood light, on the ride home she asked, "How is Anna liking kindergarten?"

"She's in the same classroom we were, but it looks nothing the same. Computers. Laptops. Whiteboards." As Luke described the changes in kindergarten, Shelby's mind wandered. Would he describe her as Aunt Shelby to Anna's friends? Could she handle him bringing a date to Christmas?

Shelby's thoughts jumbled the closer they got to Beaumont. Like Scarlett O'Hara's "tomorrow is another day," she knew the future would take care of itself whether she liked it or not. Fate would work things out.

Even if up to this point, fate had run them ragged. Still, she and Luke had cleared this hurdle, so that boded well, right? Luke parked behind the art gallery. "For a four-strike day, the ending wasn't too bad."

"No, it was great." The interior lights flooded the cab as Shelby exited. Her camera bag dangled next to her hip.

"Shall I walk you over?" Luke asked.

While she liked the idea of spending a few more minutes with him, he had obligations upstairs. "No, go free up your babysitter. It's almost eight and a school night."

"True. Anna's usually asleep by eight thirty. I try to read her a bedtime story each night. Do you want to come up and see her?"

Luke stood near enough that she could feel his breath on her cheek, and despite the weight of the bag, Shelby had an overwhelming urge to hug him. She wanted to feel his arms around her. Press herself against his chest until the outside world dropped away.

"No. Tell her I said hi." Shelby threaded through the gap between the buildings, Luke on her heels. Rather than stopping to use the back stairs or even entering through the side door, he followed her to the curb. With the festival over, Main Street was empty. A misty haze formed halos around the streetlights, casting a mysterious glow. With the street still closed until morning, no cars drove by. The historic buildings stood tall against the night. Shelby removed her camera to shoot the slumbering block. "I'll add the ghost tours to my article."

She made an artistic shot of a stack of trash bags waiting for a pickup, the discarded remains a testament to what once was. The symbolism didn't escape her. She checked the photos on the LCD display. Angled it so Luke could see. "Like it never was."

"Nice. You captured the spookiness."

A small chill washed over her, as if the Woman in White had walked past unseen. Most likely it was the cold front moving through. "That's what I was going for. I pick what I send to my editor and she chooses from there."

Far off, an owl hooted twice. She tucked the camera back into the bag. "That's my cue."

"I'll see you Tuesday. Don't be a stranger," Luke said.

Impulsively she put her hand on his cheek. He leaned into her palm and she felt how the day's rough stubble mixed with his skin's smooth texture. "Don't worry. I won't."

"Shelby." He captured her hand, making her eyes widen. "Would it change anything if I kissed you?"

She drew in an anticipatory breath as Luke brought his mouth to hers, wanting the kiss as much as he did. He tasted of Angel's and familiarity, a divine combination. Her lips parted and she kissed him back. Her tongue found his, and the kiss deepened until her camera bag shifted off her shoulder and swung into his arm. She stepped back, every nerve ending sizzling. Their kisses in high school had been delicious. This had been decadent. Mind-bending. Full of unlimited promises.

"I'll see you Tuesday," she said. She forced newborn-colt legs to move. She sensed he watched her walk to the inn, but when she turned around on the front porch, she couldn't tell if he was there. She doubted it.

Shelby found her mom finishing up the next morning's breakfast prep. "Can I help?"

"You can keep me company." Her mom moved blueberry muffins from the cooling rack and into a storage container. "How was your day? Get any great photographs?"

"I did." Shelby sat at the table.

Her mom pressed the lid tight and it made a click. "How's Luke?"

"Good. We ate at Angel's."

"And afterward?" Her mom moved the sealed container to a shelf in the open pantry.

"I walked home."

Her mom washed her hands and started to empty the dishwasher. Plate in hand, she turned and arched an eyebrow. "You forget I own an inn. I feed newlyweds breakfast. Your lips are swollen. Queso doesn't cause puffiness."

"Fine. He kissed me." Shelby told her mom about both Maren and flying *Playgroup*.

"Doesn't that beat all." Her mom dropped into the chair next to Shelby. She put her hand on Shelby's knee. "How are you feeling about all this?"

"I don't know. It doesn't matter. I'm leaving. It was a kiss for old time's sake." Although she knew it was more. "It's good to know he did love me and didn't cheat. But there's no way I can do long distance, even if my heart's suddenly confused."

"No, that wouldn't be fair to either of you, or Anna." Her mom patted Shelby's knee and she drew comfort from it. "Your life is traveling, not running an inn."

Shelby leaned her head on her mom's shoulder. "I feel guilty not taking over."

Her mom dropped her arm and Shelby snuggled close. "Your father and I know this isn't your dream. When it's time for us to retire, we'll hire a manager or sell to someone who will run the inn the way we have. You and Luke were kids when you talked about following in our footsteps. Everyone knows childhood dreams are designed to fire your imagination. They are things you try out and discard until you find the right fit. Photography is your fit. You make your father and me so proud. So very proud. Every single day."

Shelby's eyes moistened. "I want to make you proud."

"You do. And now that the truth is out, maybe you'll come home for the holidays. I loved seeing some of the places you brought us, but don't think I didn't know what you were doing, jet-setting all over so you didn't have to be here and face him."

"It would have been awkward, especially with how close our families are. I couldn't face seeing them together. Or watch her lord over the fact he loved her instead of me. Then it became habit to be somewhere else every holiday and have you join me."

Her mom stroked her hair. "He's happier than I've ever seen him since he's moved back. And even more so since you've become friends again."

Shelby used her sleeve to wipe her eyes. "Can we fix Dad and Mr. Thornburg next?"

Her mom didn't seem too concerned. "They'll come around."

"At least you and Mrs. Thornburg aren't sneaking around like me and Luke."

"No, but we haven't been able to visit as much as we'd like. Marriage is complicated, and if your father needs me to have his back, then I have his back. That's what love is."

Tight in her mom's embrace, Shelby wiggled closer. "I might be spending more time with Luke. After all, I'm flying."

"Don't worry. Your secret is safe with me. For the town and for your assignment, I'll run interference."

"Thanks. I hate deceiving them, but it's best."

"Don't give them a second thought. Their silliness has dominated enough of our lives."

Shelby straightened, gave her mom a kiss and went upstairs. She unpacked her camera, then uploaded and scrolled through the photos. She had dozens of images of Luke and, on impulse, she texted him some of the shots, then got a quick reply.

These are great. Thanks!

Welcome.

She got another text back. I'm not sorry I kissed you.

Shelby wasn't, either. She touched her lower lip. Studied a photo of Luke. Noted the way the light danced in his eyes and how the angle highlighted the strength of his jaw. She'd once traced that dip in his chin. He'd aged well, matured like fine wine, and become a great dad. He was the whole package.

The perfect man. The tug on her heartstrings grew stronger. She prepared for bed and climbed beneath the covers. He was all she'd ever dreamed of; now, he was even more. In a sense, nothing stood between them. No misunderstandings. No lies. Nothing but a matter of two thousand miles and two different lives and careers. Best to guard her heart, which beat a little faster whenever she thought of the potential unleashed in that kiss.

She texted him three words. See you Tuesday.

Chapter Seven

Tuesday afternoon, Shelby walked north on Main Street to Caldwell's. She'd walked by the shuttered bar yesterday when she'd gone on a camera scavenger hunt around the neighborhood. She'd decided on an alphabet challenge. For *A*, she'd photographed a ceramic-apple pencil holder, perfect for a teacher's desk in News and Notables, a gift shop located in the building that was once the first print shop west of the Missouri River.

For *B*, she'd gone to the bookstore, shooting the rows of books on the sales shelves. For *C*, she'd gone back to Auntie Jayne's Cookies, because who didn't want a chocolate-chip cookie? For *D*, she'd shot the street sign dividing North Main from South Main, and for *E*, the elephant-ears hosta plants that were starting to show the first signs of wilt. And so on, including a toy xylophone for X. She still couldn't believe Luke had taken a photography class so he could understand her better, and wondered if his professor had had him find a photo for all twenty-six letters.

She'd also helped her mom make a lemon-meringue pie. While she wasn't certain she'd be able to recreate the tart pie or fluffy egg-white topping on her own, she'd still experienced a sense of accomplishment when the meringue didn't fall. And the end result had been delicious.

Caldwell's had brown paper covering the windows, so she texted Luke and he opened the front door. His beaming smile gave her tingles from head to toe. "Hey," he greeted. "How was your day?"

"Good."

If they'd been dating, he would have kissed her. After Sunday night, she'd analyzed their kiss, mulling it over and over. Now she studied him, noticing he had a white T-shirt underneath a long-sleeve, plaid button-down. The sleeves were rolled up, revealing the soft hairs on his forearms. He had drywall residue on his jeans. His delicious scent mixed with a hint of sawdust. "Let me show you around."

She stepped into the huge space that had once served as the main bar. Everything had been gutted. The walls had been stripped down to studs and three workmen were rewiring the electrical. Overhead beams needing additional supports received sistering. A crew of two were sanding and refinishing barn doors.

Open blueprints were lying on a piece of plywood on top of two sawhorses. Shelby walked over and took a peek. "What's a makerspace?"

"It's a community space with tools and manufacturing equipment. Makerspaces are designed to give crafters access to resources and tech they wouldn't have otherwise. Like, we'll have a kiln, pottery wheels and several computers and 3D printers. We'll have looms, tech spaces and art areas. A darkroom." He pointed to the plans. "That's here."

He flipped a page. "Upstairs we're expanding the kitchen with commercial equipment. I've secured grants allowing for people of all incomes to call this place theirs. Think of a makerspace like an idea incubator. We're standing in the flex room. Envision rows of chairs for how-to lectures or filled with tables for craft events."

She glanced around, mentally forming pictures. But her strength was seeing things already there and she found the vision in Luke's mind outside her reach. "Sounds impressive and wonderful."

Talking about his project made him energetic. His brightened eyes and excited tone were infectious. "It's a gamble, but the business plan is solid."

"What does your dad think?"

Luke gave a slight shrug. "I haven't told him the full details. He's a silent partner. We decided on a hundred dollars a month rent until I make a profit, then he gets fifteen percent until our negotiated purchase price is paid. I invested the rest. I have enough set aside so I can forgo a salary for about six months. It should support me after that."

A worker carrying a sheet of drywall approached, and Shelby stepped out of the way. "Those are generous terms."

"They are but he's staying out of it and letting me do it on my own. I needed something all me, you know?"

"I get it. That's why these photo spreads are so important."

Luke led her down a hall. "This space will be the darkroom. What do you think?"

Studs framed out a room with an extra deep opening—one designed to accommodate a light-blocking, revolving-doorway system. "I appreciate your attention to detail. I always liked the darkroom. It's becoming a lost skill."

"I found a teacher who is willing to do a series of beginner classes. Each one of our makerspaces will have a resident artist, builder or creator. I plan to feature local artists and their work. I don't have any pieces for the walls yet, but as you can tell, drywall and plumbing are priorities if we're to open the first weekend in November."

"I can help you with the walls. Tell me the sizes and I can have some of my photos mounted as canvases. I've got a place in Seattle that does it for me. I donate things all the time."

"Thank you." He rewarded her with a killer smile and she felt its impact down in her toes. "You never cease to amaze me."

"It's nothing." She bloomed under his attentions. What would it be like to have him smile at her like that every day? He had once, and she'd loved him for it. "In fact, you could auction them when done and use the proceeds to start a scholarship for needy students. Art shouldn't be only for the privileged."

"That's part of my business plan. Your generosity will let me accelerate that portion. Thank you. I'm overwhelmed and grateful." He and Shelby stood close, his delicious aftershave permeating her senses as if whispering sweet nothings.

She could stay in his sexy and magical aura forever, but they separated as Lisa and Carl came through the back entrance. Lisa called, "Hey, you two! We flying or what?"

"You know it," Luke called. He told the foreman he was leaving for the day, and Shelby rode shotgun with Carl and Lisa in the back seat. After a detour to retrieve *Playgroup*, Luke drove about thirty miles west, into the closest state park, where a large, dry and cut floodplain made a perfect launch site. A few round bales lined the edges of the field, but those wouldn't be in the way. Shelby had already checked the weather, and there was no chance of rain until later in the week. The skies were clear and blue.

Luke and Carl dragged the bag out of the trailer while Shelby and Lisa removed the basket and the burner equipment.

Once the fabric and lines were out of the bag, Lisa and Carl spread out the envelope. Made of nylon panels called gores, the balloon lifted when the gores expanded because of the hot air. *Playgroup*'s solid-colored orange skirt was made of a flame-resistant material like the kind used by firemen. The skirt was the narrow part closest to the burners.

Playgroup's crown, or top, consisted of heavier material with a silicone coating designed to protect the envelope from both high heat and fungi. The crown was orange with yellow triangles, forming a sunburst when viewed from overhead. Below that, *Playgroup* had an area of white before a spiraling, zigzag pattern of blue, yellow and orange circled around, with orange being the dominant color. Then came the reverse, more yellow, then blue, then white, until the pattern repeated at the skirt. *Playgroup*'s colors created a sharp contrast with the green-and-brown field. Shelby shot a few photos while Carl and Lisa arranged the envelope and attached the lines. Then she and Luke assembled the burners and the basket. "Like riding a bike," Luke said.

"At least the lines are straight," Lisa said.

Shelby's face heated, which she blamed on the

sun overhead and not the memory of the kiss she and Luke had shared.

Assembly complete, Shelby doubled-checked the burners and ensured the security of the basket cables. She checked that the four fuel cylinders were clamped into the corners and the lines connected correctly. She slid on the pair of flame-resistant leather gloves and gave Luke a thumbs-up. Excitement caused a small shiver to race through her. "Let's stand her up."

At this point, everything, including the basket, was lying on its side on the ground. Shelby stood by the basket and watched as Luke pulled the starter rope on a huge circular fan. Carl and Lisa held open the skirt and Luke directed the blast of air into the envelope. *Playgroup* began to inflate and the colorful fabric waved from the air currents.

While it would have been easier with more people to hold the skirt open, *Playgroup* made it easy, as if excited to fly after being cooped up for year. She inflated and expanded, her glorious colors on full display. At this point, Shelby fired the burners. As pilot, she was the only one legally allowed to touch them. The flame shot forth, heating the air the fan pushed into the fabric.

Being near the burners was like being next to a huge bonfire on steroids, and sweat formed and trickled down her right temple. Using the inside of her elbow, she quickly wiped it and concentrated. She had to ensure buoyancy so they didn't get a false lift.

At this point, with the air inside *Playgroup* heated, the balloon began to rise and bounce in its effort to get into the air. The basket tipped off its side and, ready for this shift, Shelby ignored the door and went up and over the wicker wall and into the open basket.

She was now underneath the skirt and controlling the burners as *Playgroup* stood up—its crown high and envelope puffed out. To keep her on the ground, Lisa and Carl held ropes, as did Luke. Shelby checked the instrumentation to ensure buoyancy. She added more heat. "Almost there."

At this point, trying to keep the balloon and basket down meant arm strength and weight. A small but curious crowd had gathered. After Carl issued directions, a few rushed forward to help hold *Playgroup* down by leaning on the basket edges. Luke climbed into the basket. Gaining sure footing, he stood near Shelby, keeping the basket weighted correctly.

She glanced at the instruments. A thrill shot through her. "Ready?"

He grinned wide. "Yeah."

Carl signaled the holders to ease their hold, and *Playgroup* lifted a foot off the ground while Luke gathered the tie-down lines and secured them. Then Shelby said, "Let her go."

As everyone stepped back, Shelby added heat. Freed from her constraints, *Playgroup*'s fighting and rocking stopped immediately. She rose smoothly into the air, her rise accompanied by delighted cheers of those on the ground below.

"She seems happy," Shelby said as the ground began to fade with each whoosh of flame.

"I know I am," Luke said.

The space inside the basket seemed to shrink. Shelby studied the instrumentation, in part to ensure a safe climb and also to hide her expressions lest Luke read too much into them. She was happy, too. Flying. Luke. A perfect day. Shelby pressed the lever and released more fuel into the burners. After about five seconds, the balloon rose.

Every pilot compensated for the "five-second rule," or balloon-reaction time. Vent the crown and five seconds later the balloon would lower. Add heat and five seconds later it would rise. Since hot-air balloons traveled with the wind and the breeze was light, but steady, the ride was smooth and serene.

Playgroup coasted over the world below, with Shelby adding heat when necessary. Depending on wind direction, speed and the topography below, she kept *Playgroup* between twelve hundred and fifteen hundred feet. As in driving a car, the pilot had to become one with the vehicle, seeing all around and paying attention to all systems. Her dad had described it as flying in front of yourself.

The sun moved lower on the horizon, creating patterns of light and dark on the landscape below. She gazed into the balloon, which was like peering into a colorful cave. "I should take pictures."

"Enjoy the moment. Smile." Luke's phone was in his hand and he took her photo. "I'll send you a copy." But first, he leaned into her space. Holding his arm out, he took a photo of them together, selfie-style. "Documentation of another L-and-S adventure."

One she'd remember forever. Her phone pinged with the photos. Shelby gazed out at the bright blue sky. She studied where the ground rose up to meet the horizon line. She inhaled, smelling the mix of fresh air and propane. There was nothing else like it.

"I always forget how incredible this is," Luke said. His hands rested on the basket edge, his phone tucked safely into his jeans pocket. Trying not to be diverted by Luke's nice, shapely backside, she checked the instruments…again.

"This is why I love flying. When you're up here, it's like the world drops away. Literally." A gaggle of Canadian geese flew below them and settled onto a pond. "I didn't know I needed this."

She pushed aside how easily it would be to need him. Already he'd seeped under her skin. They'd returned to their easy companionship. And that kiss…

The wind carried them away from town and the state park, out over rural topography alternating between strips of farmland and deep forest. They flew over small streams and ponds, the water reflecting the balloon. The sun dipped lower in the sky, the angle casting *Playgroup*'s shadow on the trees below.

"Look." She pointed to a hawk diving after something, and later the horses galloping through a pasture toward a barn. They flew over mobile homes, traditional white farmhouses and some large country estates. *Playgroup* went over farms with silos and cattle, over the occasional cabin popping visible in a clearing, and she provided Luke and Shelby with a bird's-eye view of cars on rural roads, of people out in their backyards barbequing. The balloon could fly as high as three thousand feet, but Shelby stayed around eleven hundred, which provided better views of the world below. Unless descending, she kept the balloon at a thousand feet minimum.

"I forget how beautiful Missouri is," Shelby said.

"I'm sure lots of places you've seen are," Luke said. "But there's no place like home."

They'd brought a small, soft-side cooler filled with snacks, and Luke handed Shelby a colorful, reusable steel water bottle he'd uncapped. She took a long sip. "True. The world is a marvel."

"Hard to believe the sky will be full next two weekends when everyone gets here," Luke said. "We should fly at state."

The flame whooshed. Below them a family of ducks were specks in a farm pond, which reflected *Playgroup* as the balloon flew over. "What?" Had she heard him correctly?

"The entry and fuel for the state competition are paid for. If we go this Saturday, it'll give us some real practice for the town event. There's a dinner and everything. It'll give Lisa and Carl a date night."

And us, Shelby thought. "Won't word get back to your dad?"

Luke's jaw tightened. "Maybe. If it does, I'll deal with it. He's not going to have his own son arrested."

"You hope. Your dad can be scary. Remember that one time he caught us out late on my front porch. We weren't even dating yet."

They'd both been grounded for a week for breaking curfew. "Yeah, I got the sex lecture. If you're worried, we can keep *Playgroup* at Lisa and Carl's. Besides, my mom's on our side."

Shelby blinked. "She knows? I mean, I told my mom."

He grinned. "How do you think I got the key and the manual?"

He'd surprised her. Shelby couldn't help but shake her head in disbelief at the lengths he'd go. "Okay, then. We'll do it. It'll add to my story."

"There's the adventurer I know." His smile widened and she wished she could stay like this forever. Happy. But all good things ended.

"Speaking of adventures, this one's about over. We need to find a landing spot."

The sun was a fiery orange-and-yellow ball on the horizon, already dipping below so it fast appeared like a glowing semicircle. "Three more minutes to enjoy our view."

"I'll let Carl and Lisa know." Luke secured the water bottle and sent a text.

Shelby worked the lines, venting to let hot air escape so *Playgroup* slowly descended. She consulted the instruments and GPS. Off in the distance, she could see a huge, empty field with hay bales lining one side. A two-lane, paved highway ran parallel, meaning their chase vehicle would have easy access. She pointed. "There."

Glancing at the GPS, Luke texted his sister the coordinates. Shelby vented the gores, controlling the descent so *Playgroup* lowered smoothly, easily clearing the tops of the trees surrounding the field. She expelled more air, targeting a spot in the center.

Like when she flew a plane, the ground rose to greet her. The basket touched down perfectly, but then as sometimes happened, the envelope dragged and the basket bounced. She vented more air and set the basket down. She turned off the burners. Expelling more air, the envelope crumpled. As *Playgroup* deflated, the combination of an unsteady basket on uneven ground and envelope drag caused the basket to tip, and over she and Luke went, tumbling into the soft field grass.

Luke fell out on his back, and she landed face-down on top Luke, who caught her with a muffled "Ooff."

Behind the basket, *Playgroup*'s colorful fabric fluttered and settled to the ground, spent. Inches above him, her gloved hands pressed into the earth. "I'll have to work on sticking the landing."

Luke grinned and reached to brush some hair off her face. "Although, the view's not so bad from here."

Time froze, as it had their final New Year's Eve. Luke's brown eyes blinked at her. She hadn't worn a ponytail today, and her hair fell around her face. He smelled divine—his unique scent mixed with the smell of sweet, freshly cut hay. Her body, pressed against the full length of his, met his arousal with her own.

He flicked a soft thumb over her cheek. "Hey there."

"Hey." She would die if she didn't kiss him again.

He met her halfway, in a soft, gentle kiss that became increasingly more urgent the longer his mouth remained joined to hers. No one kissed like Luke. She'd experimented, she knew. His hands threaded into her hair and they melted together. She heard herself say his name, a whispered sigh. The sun dipped low, bathing them in soothing, seductive shadows. Orange and reds burst across the western sky.

A loud series of honks cut across the field and shattered the moment—the staccato of short and long honks signaling the arrival of Luke's truck and their chase crew. Headlights swept across the field, and before the crew reached their location, Shelby broke off the kiss and clambered to her feet. Luke stood and brushed the loose grass off his jeans. Carl pulled onto the shoulder and threw on the hazard lights.

"Sorry it took us so long!" Lisa yelled out the window.

"No problem," Luke called gruffly.

Rattled by the fact her lips still tingled and craved more, Shelby kept her chin tucked and began to disassemble the burners. The four of them made quick work of packing *Playgroup* and soon drove off.

"How was it?" Lisa asked from the back seat.

Luke merged onto the rural highway. "Great."

By the time they arrived back at Caldwell's, Carl and Lisa had agreed to crew both the state race events. They retrieved their car and waved as they drove off. Then Luke drove to his apartment and parked behind the building. "Would you like to come up?"

Yes. But instead of voicing that thought, Shelby shook her head. "You have to get Anna."

"I'd like to kiss you again," Luke said.

She wanted that, too. "Probably not wise."

He tucked some hair behind her ear. "Your leaving doesn't change how much I enjoy kissing you."

They sat in the truck, which was softly lit by the alley's dusk-to-dawn light. He ran his thumb over her cheek, and for a moment she allowed herself to rest her cheek in his palm. Then she lifted her head, smiled wistfully and opened the truck door, grateful the overhead light didn't come on and show the conflicting emotions dancing across her face. She wanted another kiss, which would be an absolute mistake.

"So, Friday?" Shelby asked, purposely making her tone light and casual as Luke joined her in the alley.

"Yep." He shoved his hands into his jean pockets and shifted his weight. "Thank you for doing this."

As they walked back toward his parents' building and the inn, she knew she couldn't keep letting him feel beholden. "Stop that. I'm not some superhero. I'm enjoying being here more than I thought I would. I've enjoyed spending time with you. And flying," she added quickly. "I'll have to rethink some of the shots I'd planned. Tonight gave me a new perspective. On a lot of things." She'd wanted him to kiss her. Enjoyed being pressed against him. Wondered what it would be like to touch him skin-to-skin. Craving him came so easily. They'd been together longer than they'd been apart.

All the pent-up feelings she'd had since forever threatened to burst forth. He was such a good guy. She'd met all types traveling, and Luke was a rare breed. Sincere. Special. Soul-mate stuff.

The streetlight between their parents' houses flickered. Over at the inn, her dad stepped out to address guests sitting on the porch. Shelby backed away from Luke. "Good night."

"Good night, Shelby. Sleep well." Luke turned and

made his way to his parents' front door. She headed up her front walk and nodded at the guests enjoying the evening before entering the brightly lit foyer. Her dad walked in from the parlor. "Hey, Shelby. Just getting home?"

"Yep. I was out with Luke." She followed her dad into the kitchen.

"Don't let him stab you in the back like he did before. He's a chip off the old block," her dad warned.

Shelby sighed. "Dad, I love you and thank you for caring, but you're wrong. Ask Mom to fill you in. And you and Mr. Thornburg really need to hash things out and be adults."

"We tried. I'm lucky he didn't pour beer on me at Miller's."

She bit her lip and held her ground. "If you and Mr. Thornburg want to be at each other's throats, fine. But leave me and Luke out of it. And you're hurting Mom."

Her dad opened the refrigerator and removed a caffeine-free soda. "She's on my side."

Shelby understood her mom's frustration. "It's not about sides. It's about friendship. Go read Robert Frost's 'Mending Wall.' I'd say both you and Mr. Thornburg are 'old-stone savage armed' and being quite foolish."

He poured a glass of tea. "Putting your English minor to good use, I see."

"Read it." Shelby turned toward the stairs, her

points almost all delivered. "And Luke's a good guy. Seriously, life is too short to hold on to anger."

"When did you get so smart?" Her dad pulled the tab of his pop can.

"It's common sense." Shelby gave him a kiss good-night. "And I'm figuring some things out myself."

After getting Anna home and settled into bed with her teddy bear tucked under her arm, Luke poured himself a glass of water and took a long drink. He'd kissed Shelby again. She'd tumbled into his arms, smelled so sweet and felt so good. Her mouth had curved just so, and her hair draped like silk over her cheeks, the blue highlights shimmering. The setting sun had cast a soft light on her face, illuminating her eyelashes and adding a subtle shimmer to her eyes. She'd met him halfway. The kiss had been a taste of heaven. A force of nature.

If they hadn't heard the horn, how far would they have gone? His desire hadn't abated. If anything, he wanted her even more. He put the glass in the dishwasher, set a detergent pod inside and pressed the button for the normal cycle. The machine hummed. Luke turned off the overhead lights.

The mundane nature of the chores struck him as funny, but his subsequent laugh came out as more of a harsh cough. What did he have to offer Shelby? He was a widowed dad rehabbing a building, opening a business and developing roots. She was a global adventure photographer. She'd been to over one hundred countries and five continents. She lived in hipster Seattle. No wonder she seldom visited boring Beaumont except for several days each year. She wouldn't even be staying if not for her magazine spreads. His head knew the truth—they had no future—but his heart didn't care.

He'd been a good husband to Maren, after he'd finally agreed to date her. But he'd never shared with her the deep, instinctive connection he'd had with Shelby, as if he and Shelby were two halves forged by fate to create one perfect whole. He was himself when he was around her—he didn't pretend to be anyone else or feel pressured to work in a career he didn't enjoy. When Shelby smiled, his entire heart and mind—even the darkest corners—filled with light.

She'd take a piece of his heart with her when she left two weekends from now, which seemed a fair penance for his not being man enough to trust in her love long ago. He certainly didn't deserve it now. He climbed into bed and tried to sleep.

About five minutes later, his bedroom light flipped on and Anna stood in the doorway. "Dad? I had a bad dream."

"It's okay. Come here." He lifted the covers, letting her crawl under. She curled next to him, tossing her arm over his T-shirt. He stroked her hair until she fell back asleep. Then he gently lifted her up and put her back in her bed, smoothing out her nightgown and tucking her teddy bear safely under her arm. His life was raising Anna and opening a business in Beaumont.

Shelby belonged to the world. He'd never find anyone else like her. But no matter what happened over the next two weeks, she was leaving. It would be unfair to ask her to stay.

With a sense of finality, Luke clicked off the light.

Chapter Eight

By Friday afternoon, Shelby was decidedly nervous. She hadn't seen Luke since Tuesday. He was busy with Caldwell's. She'd traveled around Missouri and learned more of her mom's recipes.

She'd also culled and edited pictures for her editor. She'd agonized over which photographs to give Luke, then, finally satisfied, she'd uploaded the shots to have them made into canvas wall art. Sure, she and Luke had texted. Mostly serious race decisions. Maybe a few harmless flirtations. Enough to whet her appetite for chatting in person, perhaps more. Hard to forget his kiss.

Despite putting physical distance between them, he'd remained in her thoughts, especially the way his mouth felt on hers. She pressed fingers to her lips as the anticipation of seeing him today became more nerve-wracking than the idea of racing. The Missouri balloon race was more a festival than a serious, cutthroat competition. She'd read over the pilot information. She'd worn her lucky jeans and favorite long-sleeve, pink-toned plaid flannel. She was ready.

Tonight was the state balloon glow, where all the balloons would stand against the night like Chinese lanterns. They'd inflate *Playgroup* tomorrow, even if she remained grounded while others flew. However, Shelby itched to fly. Why not? If they were there and had the fuel? Being in the air with Luke had been magical and she wanted more. Even if, like the flight, it couldn't last.

The grandfather clock in the foyer chimed half past three, so Shelby walked to Luke's apartment. She found Lisa and Carl already outside, along with two people who would serve as takeoff crew. "Bruce and Kate," Lisa introduced. "They'll follow us."

"Nice to meet you," Shelby said.

The drive into St. Louis took a little over an hour. Upon reaching the series of ball fields being used as launching grounds, Luke followed well-marked signs to their designated spot.

The evening promised perfect temperatures and clear skies. Whether they'd launch tomorrow remained to be seen as a front approached. One thing every Missourian knew was the phrase "Don't like the weather, wait five minutes and it'll change." Missouri could go—and had, on many occasions—from eighty degrees to thirty-two in fewer than thirty minutes. While the TV weather forecasters were pretty accurate, if some unsettled weather came up from the Gulf of Mexico, tomorrow could be iffy.

The wind wouldn't be a problem once in the air— the balloon moved with the wind and the ride remained smooth. However, all sorts of variables came into play depending on the wind direction and topography. Pilots either couldn't fly over or land on a PZ, which stood for prohibited zone. PZs could be zoos, national parks, prisons, military bases or airports. In other places, pilots couldn't go under or above certain altitudes. For instance, if the wind pushed the balloons in the state race toward the airport, they'd either have to be above or below the flight path of any incoming planes.

"Hey, I know you." Shelby turned as she heard a voice. It was the pilot from Iowa, Caleb Munson. "John Bien's daughter. Is he here?" Caleb glanced around.

"Nope." Shelby pointed to the button pinned to her shirt. "I'm the pilot."

"Well, I'll be. That's great. Next generation taking over. Tell your dad I said hi."

"Appreciate it and will do." Luke approached as Caleb walked away. Shelby filled him in. "Remember when I said I chased the balloon in Iowa? It was his."

The recognition continued at the pilot's briefing.

"Luke? Shelby?" a familiar-looking woman said. "It *is* you. Look at how much you've grown. And flying. Your dads must be so proud."

And she was only the first of many.

"I forgot how tight-knit the balloon community is. Everyone knowing everyone," Luke said as they returned to *Playgroup* after the briefing.

"Clearly. I can't believe people remember us from being kids. I don't even recognize myself sometimes."

Some even asked if she and Luke were married or dating. That had been awkward. They found Carl, Lisa and their friends sitting in lawn chairs and enjoying a picnic. While there was a pilot-and-crew dinner afterward, owing to the hour drive, they'd decided to skip it. Before sunset, pilots and crews began to inflate and the field flurried with activity. Small crowds gathered, ebbing and flowing as balloons began to stand. As if she was ready to show off, *Playgroup* filled extra fast. Shelby stood in the basket, which remained firmly tethered to the ground, chatting with spectators. When dusk fell, the balloons performed an all-burn, which meant they glowed like oversize lanterns, with full colors on display.

Next weekend, at the Beaumont balloon glow, pilots would have specific, timed instructions for a burn schedule. They'd do flicker burns and no burns, making the balloons appear to do a choreographed sequence. From the air, at one point, the effect appeared almost like a wave. On the ground, some spectators would be thrust into blackness as the balloons briefly darkened.

Tonight, balloons glowed continuously. As the night wound on, Shelby's nerves calmed. She manned *Playgroup* and answered questions, which kept her busy. No time to be alone with Luke and her growing feelings.

She was the only one in the basket, and thickly woven wicker separated them, but that didn't stop her awareness and anticipation. She'd felt his gaze on her most of the night. When she'd catch him looking, he'd give her a secret smile that told her he was also thinking of another kiss.

She reached to fire the burner. Night had fallen and the sky twinkled with millions of stars and a bright half moon. The crowd wandering through remained steady. Older couples held hands. Younger couples pushed children in strollers. Elementary-age kids asked tons of questions. Middle-schoolers pretended to be cool, but hung on every word she said. High-schoolers hung out with friends or dates. Multiple generations made the annual event a family affair, and many stopped by to tell Shelby and Luke how many times they'd seen *Playgroup*. Everyone had a favorite balloon, and for many, it was *Playgroup*. Or maybe they said that to everyone. Either way, the attention was overwhelming. As part of their dads' crew, once her and Luke's jobs were done, they'd escaped. They'd been those teens wandering around, getting ice cream and watching the entertainment.

As pilot, Shelby remained inside the basket. She answered questions, posed for pictures and selfies, and concentrated on keeping *Playgroup* glowing. As a photographer, she worked to blend in. Tonight, everyone wanted her attention.

"It's five minutes until nine. How are you doing?" Luke asked.

"Holding up. Our dads took turns doing this. It gives me a new perspective, for sure, looking at the event from inside the basket."

"Thought you might be thirsty." He handed her an uncapped steel bottle he'd filled with water.

The breeze increased for a minute, and the basket lurched and rocked back and forth. Shelby made an adjustment. "She's raring to go."

Luke leaned his arms on the wicker edge and leaned toward her. "Balloons always want to fly. It's in their job description."

"You should restart your lessons. You can fly *Playgroup* next year."

"I'm sure our dads will be back to being friends by then. This is their thing."

A young couple approached. They carried a toddler who was holding one of those foil balloons on a plastic stick. He waved it at them, and Shelby and Luke talked to the couple until it was nine. Then she shut off the fuel and *Playgroup*, like the rest of her peers, went dark and deflated. Because the fireworks began in fifteen minutes, the field bustled with activity as all around them, crews like theirs stored balloons in custom trailers.

Some pilots and crews drove off, but others remained and stayed for the fireworks. Without the heat from the burner, Shelby grew cold and shivered. Luke took off his jacket and draped it over her shoulders. She slid her arms through, smelling his scent on the soft leather. "Thanks."

He put his hand over hers and squeezed. "No problem."

Shelby laced her fingers through his, liking how he anticipated her needs, knowing when she was cold, knowing she was thirsty. He had an innate recognition of her needs before she knew them. He was the only person she'd ever been this in-sync with. Heck, she'd had dates where the guy was on his phone most of the night and by the end, she doubted he could even recount one thing she'd said. She could get used to this.

The last fireworks exploded across the sky. Smoke settled and she rose and snapped her chair closed. The trailer with *Playgroup* already attached, Shelby put the lawn chair in the truck bed and jumped into the passenger seat. She remained mostly quiet, staring out the window as the radio blared the latest pop hits. In the back, Carl and Lisa held a whispered, undecipherable conversation, the kind couples have when they love each other and share everything.

When they reached Luke's apartment, Shelby thanked everyone. Lisa waved and called, "See you tomorrow" out the window as they drove away, leaving Shelby and Luke standing in the parking area behind his building.

"You seemed distant on the way home," Luke said, again proving how well he could read her.

"Slightly tired." Not a lie. "I didn't realize how much energy it takes to be the center of attention."

"You didn't have one minute when someone wasn't asking about *Playgroup*." Moonlight illuminated his face. He was so beautiful, and she lifted her fingers as if to touch him.

Then nerves and hesitation claimed her. "It's been a great night, but, wow. Intense. My brain is racing. I should jot down thoughts for my narrative. I guess I can do both tomorrow morning. Then again, tomorrow's busy and I want to be prepared. I'm good to walk home."

"Shelby." He caught her hand and drew her into his arms. "Come up for a while. Anna's with my parents for the weekend. We can talk. Eat a late-night snack. Let me massage your shoulders because you had one arm in the air most of the night."

His touch stoked the fire already raging. He leaned to kiss her lips, and when she caught his mouth, she devoured him and took control. By the time they parted, her chest heaved from the kiss's intensity. Her hands clung to his back. "If I come up, we won't be talking. I want you too much. I want your skin on mine. I run to danger, but I don't know if this is wise."

"I won't ask you to stay. I'm going into this with my eyes open. I know you're leaving."

She and Luke weren't casual friends. They'd loved intensely. "There's no man in every port. I've had a few relationships, nothing major. I don't sleep around. Hooking up sounds cheap."

His hand massaged the back of her neck, creating electrifying tingles. "You forget I know you. I want you just as much. Like we'll die if we don't touch. There's nothing cheap or wrong about that. About this."

He kissed her, and Shelby lost herself in the magic of his lips. This was Luke. Her first lover. She could spend tonight in his bed. Experience the heat of him. Cuddle in his arms. Revel in the passion. Let her heart lead, even if that meant following him through the door and upstairs.

His bedroom was the one closest to the back stairs. He headed down the long hall toward the living room, but Shelby stepped inside and flicked on the light. A photo of Anna rested on the dresser. Nothing of Maren. She drew a breath, the collar of Luke's jacket smelling of sandalwood and sage, masculinity and promise. Her breasts felt heavy and heat pooled low. Anticipation made her stomach butter-flies dance.

Luke returned. "I thought you were behind me."

"We've lost enough time." She began to undo the buttons on his shirt, exposing a smooth, chiseled chest. She ran her palms over it. "Whatever you were going to do, we can do it later."

His lips found hers, and then their hands were everywhere. Shelby explored his body, until Luke took control of hers through magical fingers that took her to heights never conquered. And then he was hers and she his, and they flew together to the moon and beyond.

Shattered, she clung to him afterward. He brushed her hair from her face before dropping a kiss on her lips. She could hear the thumping of his heart as it returned to normal. "That was incredible."

"It was." Nothing, even their times as kids, could compare or come close. She shifted, satiated.

He dropped another kiss, this one on her nose. "You've ruined me. It's never been like that for me."

"Me, either." Silence fell as they absorbed the intense implications.

"Come on," Luke said. "Let's get that snack."

Her stomach growled its agreement. "Do you have a shirt I can wear?"

He rose from the bed, the body of Adonis on full display. "Afraid to be naked?"

"No." Shelby stood. Back in high school, they'd

made love in an open field, and cramped in the tiny back seat of a car. They'd never stayed naked long. But she was proud of her body and the work she put in to be fit. And Luke…oh, he had nothing to worry about, boasting those long, lean muscles Italian masters preserved using oil paint. "I'm simply afraid you won't be able to resist me long enough to feed me," she teased.

Luke came around and she slapped him lightly on his firm ass and darted away. He chased and caught her, pulling her to him. "Minx. You'll pay for that."

"Really? You think so?" she dared, reaching around to grab his backside, her hands cupping and squeezing. They fell back onto the bed.

Too hungry for each other, they ate food much, much later.

In the end, they didn't fly the next day. No one did, not even the hare balloon, which always took off first. Mother Nature had other ideas.

Five percent chance of rain? By 4:30 p.m. it was a one-hundred-percent certainty, surprising everyone. An overcast race day expected to remain cloudy turned into a sudden downpour that soaked everything. For pilots and crew with envelopes ready for inflation, the rain created a mad scramble to pack balloons, ropes and baskets.

Text messages told them the race was canceled,

but that dinner was still on in the golf-course club-house, which was serving as race central.

"If we knew it was going to rain all day we could have stayed in bed," Luke whispered. They sat close on the love seat.

"Shh," Shelby warned. She sipped her wine, aware that Lisa was watching suspiciously from a love seat directly across. The lounge was cozy, with multiple seating groups, and a large, natural-gas fireplace flickered in the corner.

Lisa lifted her glass of cabernet from the coffee table and addressed Shelby. "I suppose it rains all the time in Seattle."

"Its nickname is the Rain City. And it is frequently gray. Mostly it's fall and winter when a light rain falls."

Carl did an online search. "Says here summer is mostly dry. There are fifty-eight days of sun per year and then one hundred and fifty rainy days."

Lisa shuddered. "So almost half a year of rain. Absolutely not for me."

Shelby sipped her Riesling. "I don't notice it. I'm gone too much."

Carl read his phone. "Says here Beaumont gets one hundred and five days of rain a year. So Seattle gets almost two months more. We get two hundred and five days of sun."

"What about snow?" Shelby asked Carl. "How does that compare?"

Carl's thumbs moved. "Let me see. We get an average of sixteen inches of snow to their four-point-six. And they only get thirty-eight inches of rain. We get forty-two."

"Huh," Lisa said. "Maybe it wouldn't be so bad there."

"Don't you start talking about humidity," Carl warned his wife, which made them all laugh. Tolerating Missouri summer humidity was considered a rite of passage.

"Sorry your pictures washed out," Lisa said.

"I got good pictures of everyone scrambling to put away their balloons." Once they'd stored *Playgroup*, Shelby had put plastic bags over her lens and camera and shot Luke, Bruce and Carl helping others still battling to get their balloons packed.

"Mother Nature wins and we'll try again next year."

Shelby sipped her wine, aware of how close Luke's leg was to hers. The event wouldn't be rescheduled, and most likely she wouldn't be here next year. "Changing weather is part of the game, so it's good to have captured that. I just feel bad we forgot to tell Bruce and Kate to bring a change of clothes."

"They'll be okay. However, I won't be if I'm in your magazine looking like a wet dog," Lisa warned.

"And as long as it doesn't rain next weekend," Luke said.

Shelby gave him a playful slap on his upper arm. "Don't jinx it."

"Hey." He grabbed her hand in his. "No worries. It's only rained once."

"True," Lisa said. "The Woman in White keeps bad weather away race weekend."

Shelby frowned. "Really? I've never heard that. But it would make interesting folklore for my story."

"It's why they picked the date," Lisa said. "Besides being the weekend after state, the first race occurred on her wedding anniversary. Now, the race isn't on the same date every year because it sticks to the weekend, but since 1975 it's only rained once."

"Fascinating. Cheers to no more rain." Shelby took a sip to hide her reaction. Luke had shifted, and his thigh pressed against hers, sending steady heat.

They talked until called for dinner, and their foursome joined a family of six at a table for ten. Waiters served food and dessert, and after she finished a huge piece of chocolate cheesecake, Shelby pushed away the empty plate. "I can't eat another bite."

"It was good," Luke agreed. He and Shelby were the only ones left at their table. Carl and Lisa were on the dance floor getting down to some upbeat pop song. He followed her gaze out to them. Carl was performing the world's worst sprinkler move ever, and Lisa was laughing with him as if neither had a care in the world.

"They seem happy," Shelby and Luke both said in unison.

"Jinx!" they said together. This made them laugh.

"This reminds me a bit of their wedding," Luke said.

"Except I wore a dress." Shelby automatically rubbed her fingers on her jeans.

"A pretty one, too. Light blue with a lace overlay of flowers. Not tomboyish, like your T-shirts and jeans."

Her eyes widened. He remembered all that?

He stood. "Shall we work off the cheesecake? Because I would love to get you in my arms again."

Shocked that he could remember her outfit all these years later, she gladly took his hand. She'd barely remembered it herself, until he reminded her. After last night, she wanted to be in his arms. They joined Lisa and Carl for the last twenty seconds of a slow number. Luke hardly had his arms around her when the DJ played an up-tempo song. Thwarted, Luke rolled his eyes.

She swayed to the rhythm, and then the crowd cheered and clapped as the song ended. The DJ began a slower number, and all around them couples moved together. Luke held out his hands, and as if a super magnet was pulling her toward him, she stepped into his arms. "I can't wait to get you alone again tonight," he whispered.

"Me, either."

He drew her close and she pressed her cheek against his chest. Despite the steady bass vocals of the male singer, Shelby swore she could hear Luke's heartbeat, as she had all those years ago. Would they have danced like this at prom? Close together, with his arms circling her waist and his hands rubbing on her lower back? Would they have felt the same anticipation, knowing of the lovemaking to come?

The DJ extended one slow song into two, and Shelby let herself go. It was heaven in his arms. He'd always be her dream man, and last night had destroyed her for anyone else. Two becoming one had taken on new meaning. If only she could stay in his arms and let this dream last forever. *Play another slow song and then another*, she wished. As she nestled closer, she exhaled a soft sigh. Luke responded by splaying his fingers and pulling her even closer. She felt safe, cherished and special. But the song ended, as all good things do, and the DJ called out to the crowd, "Let's speed things up again."

Laughing, she pushed aside the moment, threw her arms into the air and danced. For once, she ignored her head telling her that dreams were for children and dreamers. Tonight, she didn't need to be a realist.

She danced until her feet hurt. She touched Luke at every opportunity and kept in his orbit. When Lisa said, "We're ready when you are," the words had the same impact as the clock striking midnight.

In fact, it was midnight.

"I'm ready," Shelby agreed. Leaving the dance meant more time spent in Luke's bed. On the flip side, the more time she spent in his arms, the harder it would be to leave. As Beaumont was over an hour and a half away, she and Lisa stopped by the ladies' room. Lisa caught Shelby's gaze through the mirror.

"You're going to hurt him again, you know," Lisa said.

Her words acted like a knife and joy escaped Shelby faster than air from a tear in *Playgroup*'s envelope.

"He knows I'm leaving." She clung to that truth. After all, she couldn't stay. She had assignments to do and places to be. "He understands we're just friends."

Lisa's mouth thinned. "He'll tell you he's fine. It's what *friends*—" Lisa stressed the word "—do. But he won't be. And all of us will again have to mop up his heartbreak."

Lisa turned her back and hit the button on the air dryer, the noise ending all conversation. But her words had hit home. Shelby's reflection revealed the expectant, happy light had dimmed in her eyes, and when she exited the bathroom, she knew Luke noticed by the way his forehead wrinkled.

Carl and Lisa drew Luke and Shelby into conversation and the group talked the entire way home. Carl had volunteered to dry *Playgroup* so it didn't get moldy, so they dropped the trailer at Lisa and Carl's house, leaving Lisa behind. Carl rode back to get his truck, and as the two men climbed out of Luke's vehicle, Shelby grabbed her camera bag. "Ready?" Luke asked.

An hour ago, she wouldn't have hesitated. She wanted more like last night. Dancing with Luke had her body humming with anticipation. But on the drive home, she'd felt Lisa's words pierce her soul. One night of lovemaking could be explained as an aberration. A caving to temptation. To the past. A second night wiped away any and all excuses. It signified a relationship, and the only relationship Shelby and Luke could have was one of friendship. Sex would complicate that. It already had.

"I'm sorry. I ate something and it's not sitting. Rain check."

He didn't buy her reasons. "Shelby."

If she stayed, she wouldn't leave. Not in the morning. Not ever. But she didn't want to get into that with him now, or admit to herself the truth of her warring feelings. Better to leave, which was something she excelled at doing. "We'll talk tomorrow. Gotta go." Before he could accompany her, she rushed home.

Even though it was almost two, Shelby found her mom in the kitchen. She gave her a kiss. "You're up late."

"Had a late check-in. Poor dears' plane was six hours late and they almost missed their connection.

I set them up with a sandwich-and-dessert tray. How was your night? I wasn't expecting you."

Shelby didn't bury the lead. "Luke and I danced. And Lisa warned me off. So I came home because she's right."

"Come here." She wrapped her arms around Shelby, who tried not to cry. "Not sure you'll welcome my advice, but you have to follow your heart."

That was the problem. "It doesn't matter what my heart or my head want. Both are part of my body, and I have assignments lined up for the next six months. I've worked so hard to get where I am. If I stay with him tonight, stay again, it'll make things even more complicated than they already are. I can't do this again. I'm sure that he knows I wasn't sick but he's too polite to call me out. That's the kind of guy he is. I'm afraid of hurting him again when I leave." *I'm afraid I'll hurt when I leave.*

"He's lucky to have a sister who cares, but he's a big boy. He makes his own choices. Things have a way of working out."

"I'm not sure I actually believe that. It just sounds good whenever I say it."

Because, if things had really worked out, Maren never would have come between them. Then again, had she not, would Shelby have become the photographer she was today? She'd had to write a research paper in college on Robert Frost's "The Road Not Taken." Most took the poem's theme as to mean that taking the other, equally good path made everything turn out for the better.

But the deeper analysis revealed regret. What would have happened to the narrator, had the first path been chosen? Could it have been better than the second path? The poem showed how people rewrote their personal histories—how they retold their past choices to justify their current reality, as if they'd intended the results the choice brought.

Shelby's reality was eating take-out food in an apartment she hated. Travel was like a drug—it kept her high on life and let her escape hard truths. Everyone thought her job was glamorous and exciting, but her career meant having few real friends. When in Seattle, she didn't visit with friends. Instead, she read books, worked out and ran, then counted the days until her next flight. The very nature of her job meant people moved in and out of her life with increasing frequency and zero permanence. She immersed herself in her assignment location and left when finished. If she had a social-media account, it would be filled with people she'd met once.

She climbed the stairs, deciding that she must be in a funk if she was thinking of poetry this much. How many emotionally wrought poems had she written, most of them about her changing feelings for Luke? Volumes.

Melancholy and nostalgia made for strange bedfellows. Wound up, she began to process her pictures.

As she tucked herself into bed around 3:00 a.m., she concluded Beaumont was a powerful magnet not wanting to let her go.

After a dreamless sleep, and to stave off the tentacles clutching at her the longer she stayed, Shelby rose late Sunday morning. She answered Luke's questioning text with a brief "working, chat later" and devoted herself to her craft. She wrote captions. Attempted to start the accompanying feature story. Abandoning the draft, she moved to the third-floor couch. Boba slept curled against her hip as Shelby cropped, color-adjusted and filled in file information. The windows were open, and a fresh fall breeze flipped the lace curtains.

Today was sunny and beautiful. Fall really was the best time in Missouri, but aside from leaving for her morning run, Shelby remained inside and focused. She stopped only to eat, stretch her legs and visit with her parents. She'd put in hours' worth of work by dinnertime.

As if trying to get Shelby somewhat out of the house, her mom served dinner on the back porch. Shelby's mouth watered upon smelling pork roast, garlic mashed potatoes and steamed fresh green beans. A side salad and homemade bread served as accompaniments.

"Looks delicious. I'll need to run ten miles to work all this deliciousness off."

"And pie for dessert," her dad said, passing over the meat platter.

"How's the spread coming?" her mom asked.

Shelby used the serving fork and transferred sliced pork onto her dinner plate. "Great. I sent my editor a bunch of things. In fact, my editor texted she's coming to see me work. Remember how I told you she might? She's arriving Tuesday."

"We'll put her in the third-floor guest room," her dad said.

"It'll be nice to meet her after hearing so much about her over the years," her mom added. Plates full, they bowed their heads and her dad led grace.

Shelby was four bites in when the gate between their house and the Thornburgs' banged. Anna came running into view. She stopped short. "You're eating."

"Come on up," Shelby's mom called.

Anna came through the screen door. "I'm not supposed to bother people when they're eating."

"That rule's not for family or next-door neighbors and you're pretty much both." Shelby's mom patted the empty seat next to her. "Did you eat?"

"Just some chicken-noodle soup and grilled cheese. We took Grandma out for brunch."

"I'm sure she enjoyed that." Shelby's mom went inside and returned with a dinner plate and silverware. She set them in front of Anna and began to serve food onto her plate. "It's not your grandma's birthday or anniversary, though."

"It was Dad's idea. We took her just because." Anna lifted a fork and dug into the mashed potatoes.

Shelby's ears perked up. "Does your dad know you're here?"

Anna shook her head. "He's at Caldwell's. I've been at Grandma's all weekend. I told her I was going outside. She said fine."

"Won't she worry about you if you aren't in the yard?" Shelby asked.

"She knows I come over here all the time, or at least I used to. But you're here so it'll be okay." Anna took a few bites, then said, "Can you take more pictures with me?"

Shelby's heartstrings felt the tug. "Maybe tomorrow after school?" Shelby offered.

"Okay." Then as if remembering her manners, she added, "Thank you."

While they ate, Anna kept up her chatter, telling them about a chapter book she was reading. Shelby didn't mind Anna being the center of attention. It diverted her from having to mull over her feelings for Luke. They lingered around the edges of her brain, as if an eager chorus was telling her there were no real reasons they couldn't be together. Already, Shelby was second-guessing last night's decision.

Dessert was fresh-baked apple pie served with both whipped cream and vanilla-bean ice cream.

Shelby's fork cut easily through the flaky crust. She gave a deep sigh of appreciation as warm, tart apples and cinnamon filling mixed with the cold, delicious ice cream.

The gate banged and a familiar baritone voice called, "Is there enough for me?"

"Luke, of course. You know you don't even have to ask. Get in here," her mom called, bustling inside for another plate.

Butterflies hatched in Shelby's stomach and she wrung the napkin hidden in her lap. Luke was wearing jeans and a mustard-colored chambray shirt with two pockets on the chest. His hair was pushed back from his forehead, and he caught her gaze as he stepped onto the porch. She nodded slightly and bent her head to study her pie.

Luke took Anna's chair and put her on his lap. Shelby shifted, glad he sat across from her. Her mom returned with a slice. "No one makes like apple pie like you," Luke said. He put a forkful in his mouth and groaned. "So good."

"It was really good, Dad," Anna agreed. Only crumbs and a smear of melted ice cream remained on her plate.

Luke dug in. "Thanks, Mrs. B."

"How's the building coming?" her dad asked. "I read the commissioner's report. It's a unique idea. I understand you not wanting to make a fuss until the opening, but you can tell me."

"The contractors are making excellent progress. I was there today doing my part." Luke began explaining the makerspace concept and how several artisans had already signed leases. "During my research, I found that for many artists, the purchase of equipment needed to manufacture their pieces, such as kilns, is cost-prohibitive, especially when they are first starting out."

Knowing most of this already from her discussions with Luke, Shelby half listened, her concentration instead fixed on the movements of Luke's lips and the pride evident in his tone. He spoke enthusiastically. Her heart swelled. Then deflated. He was a good guy. He belonged here.

Unlike her.

The differences were stark. If she could escape inside, she would, but she'd appear rude. Or, worse, like she couldn't be around him after what had happened between them. When her mom pinned Shelby with a quick lift of her eyebrows, Shelby shifted but stayed put.

"Anna?" Upon hearing her grandfather's voice and the gate open, Anna straightened.

Luke shifted his daughter to face him. "Did you tell Grandpa where you were going?"

Anna's chin jutted out. "I told Grandma I was going outside. I'm outside."

"Technically you're inside," Luke pointed out.

"Dad." Anna added an exaggerated eye roll. "Grandma knows I come over here all the time."

"Anna, you're wrong in not telling Grandma and Grandpa you were leaving the yard." Luke's tone had quieted and Anna squirmed under his disapproval. "You need to apologize."

Shelby watched as Luke disciplined his daughter by waiting silently.

"Okay, I'm sorry," Anna blurted. Her lips quivered, but she didn't cry.

"And?" Luke pressed.

"I'll tell them next time." Anna folded her arms over her chest, mollified, her cheeks puffy. "And I'll say sorry."

Luke gave her a reassuring pat on the back. "Thank you. That way Grandpa won't be scared when he finds you gone."

"Grandma knew," Anna grumbled, but Luke's warning glance silenced her. His dad came into view and saw them all sitting on the screened porch.

"Luke, you could have told me you were with her," his dad said, clearly put out. He stopped about ten feet from the porch steps.

"I'm sorry I didn't tell you where I was going," Anna told her grandfather.

Luke gave Anna a nod, indicating she'd done the right thing, and, ever the peacekeeper, Shelby's mom worked to ease the situation further. "Mike, would you like some pie?"

Shelby saw Mr. Thornburg hesitate and shift his weight. "Was checking on Anna. Luke's got her."

"It's my mile-high apple pie, and I've got ice cream and homemade whipped cream," her mom said, trying to tempt him. She held up a pie tin containing enough for three mouthwatering pieces. "Why don't you text Cynthia and tell her to come over and get a piece, too."

"It's fine, Mike," Shelby's dad added. "It's only pie."

"Maybe next time." Luke's dad backtracked and the gate clattered behind him. Shelby's dad rose and went inside.

Shelby's mom smiled wistfully at Luke and Shelby. "Well, some progress is better than none. No immediate yelling."

The wind chimes tinkled, and Shelby's mom carried the pie pan inside. She came back with a plastic container filled with the extra pieces and set it in front of Luke. "Drop those off on your way home."

"Yes, ma'am." Luke rose and picked up the container. "That's our cue, Anna. Tell everyone 'bye."

"'Bye, everyone." Anna hugged Mrs. Bien before turning to Shelby and wrapping her arms around her. Anna squeezed tight. "Love you, Shelby." Then Anna let go and darted off, the door clattering behind her.

Shelby stood rooted. She'd had other children hug her. It was an impulsive, sweet gesture. Children loved everyone. Right?

Her shaken gaze connected with Luke's. His lips curved gently upward. He knew, but didn't acknowledge, and said simply, and softly, "Good night, Shelby."

Something broke inside Shelby and tore at her heart as she watched Anna and Luke walk away. Noticing her choking up, her mom gave Shelby's hand an understanding squeeze and went inside. Shelby carried in the remaining plates.

"She's a sweet girl," Shelby said, successful in shutting down any waterworks before they started.

Her mom began washing dishes. "She is. She's taken quite the shine to you."

Shelby reached for a glass and filled it with water. Attempted a calming drink. "You're another grandma. I'm like the cool aunt who can teach her pictures. She's eager to learn. I'm afraid she's too attached."

"True. She'll miss you."

Shelby fought the truth—she'd miss Anna. But admitting that fact meant admitting she'd miss Luke. "Luke says I shouldn't worry. And I guess I can try to visit more."

"We'll all like that."

Shelby heard the hopefulness in her mom's words and hated it. Was grateful when her phone beeped with a message from her editor. "Jennifer is arriving Tuesday morning. We're planning on a series of day trips into St. Louis."

"You'll be busy."

Shelby opened her email. "She's never been here so she sent me a list. I'll still be sure to give Anna one more lesson." Shelby would make Anna a priority.

"She'll like that. And it's been such a blessing to have you home. Thanks for the extra time."

"You may not like being part of my article."

"Oh, we'll be fine no matter what you write. You always make us proud."

There was no recrimination. Just acceptance and love. Shelby's guilt meter began to tick. One more week. "I'll try to make it home more," she promised. "I'll at least try." Shelby leaned over and gave her mom a quick kiss. "But right now, I have to get back to work."

Chapter Nine

"You're taking me to the top of the Arch. I've enjoyed a dinner cruise on the Mississippi. You even took me up to Hannibal to the Mark Twain home. And I still haven't met the mysterious Luke," Shelby's editor, Jennifer, said on Thursday. "I'm beginning to think he doesn't exist."

"He's as real as this tram." Shelby shifted as the car lurched. She and Jennifer were in one of the five-foot-high, egg-shaped pods designed to take visitors to the top of the Gateway Arch. At 630 feet tall, it was the largest manmade monument in the Western Hemisphere and the world's tallest arch. In a high-school quiz-bowl match, Shelby had earned a point for knowing the distance between the north and south Arch legs was also 630 feet.

Jennifer gripped the edge of her seat as the car jolted. She was in the center seat, the one directly opposite the door and the one with the most headroom, with Shelby to her right. Three people they didn't know were riding with them. "Is it always like this?"

"Yep." Shelby leaned over for a selfie. "It can be a bit claustrophobic, but it's a feat of modern engineering. Each capsule makes a one-hundred-and-fifty-five-degree rotation as it climbs and descends." When they'd started at the bottom, the cars were hanging from the track. When they arrived at the top, the track was at the bottom. The reverse would occur on the way down. Four minutes later, they climbed out of the small pod, and walked up the set of stairs that led to the curved floor and the observation windows.

The space at the top contained sixteen windows a mere seven inches high and twenty-seven inches long. The view was fabulous, and Shelby took photos of downtown. From south to north, highlights included the round building that had once been a hotel, and beyond that, Busch Stadium and its adjacent Ballpark Village nightlife center.

Panning right, they saw the Thomas F. Eagleton Courthouse with the domed top, the largest federal courthouse in the country, and then the Old Courthouse, with its Federal-style architecture. She and Jennifer had toured the old building, which had four wings and massive pillars. It was the site of the infamous Dred Scott case, and before entering the museum under the Gateway Arch, they'd discussed the injustice and how the case had hastened the Civil War.

Shelby was pointing out some of the other sights when Jennifer spoke. "You still haven't answered me about Luke," she prodded.

"You'll meet him tomorrow at the glow."

Jennifer peered out another window. "I'm curious. You've talked a lot about him while we've been out, probably without realizing it. Yet, you haven't seen him once since I've been here, not even to sneak off for some race-prep time."

"We're friends, teammates. It's handled." Shelby recognized she sounded defensive. "And I'm leaving. My career comes first, so anything that might want to occur isn't fair to either of us."

Jennifer leaned over to take in the view. "His daughter's cute. I met her at the inn. She seems to like you."

"She likes photography. I wish I'd had a mentor like me when I was younger. That's all this is. Besides, he's busy with the building rehab."

"Uh-huh. How's your narrative coming?"

"Lots of notes. I'm waiting until after the race." Which sounded so much better than admitting she had writer's block. Every time she tried to type something, she couldn't find the words. As if underscoring the fact that she'd not gone home with Luke Saturday night, she and Luke hadn't exchanged but three texts all week—ones she'd initiated. And one of those had been letting him know she'd sent the photos Anna had taken during her lesson on Monday.

In order to keep them from getting hurt, he was giving them space. His actions should thrill her. She'd wanted—had asked for—professionalism and space, and he was providing it. But she missed him. She longed to call and hear his voice. Her fingers itched to text something flirtatious, or something that brought him back to her. But she hadn't. It wouldn't be fair.

She and Jennifer crossed to the eastern side of the Arch, which looked over the Mississippi River and into Illinois. This view featured the riverboats on the Missouri side and the tugboats and barges lined up on the Illinois shore. They could see the Illinois casino and the Gateway Geyser, which was turned off. Shelby pointed out a few more things, including the Amtrak train crossing the river on its journey to Chicago, and the freight trains chugging the other way on a level underneath. It was a clear day and they could see for miles.

"Stand there," Shelby instructed, and she took Jennifer's picture next to the sign containing the National Park Service logo and the words *630 feet Gateway Arch St. Louis*. She showed Jennifer the results.

"I like it. You can use it for my editor's letter for your book."

Shelby lowered the camera. "What book?"

Jennifer's face broke into an excited smile. "Your

book. The publisher and I agree it's time. The work you've done for the magazine has been fantastic. I've been impressed, and so have the higher-ups. You know the magazine publishes coffee-table books of our photographers, right?"

Shelby managed an unsteady nod and Jennifer continued. "Twice a year we go to press. Two hours ago, I received final confirmation. Next April, we're debuting a compilation of your photographs in hard cover. *Around the Globe* by Shelby Bien. What do you think?"

Shocked, Shelby would have dropped her camera if the strap hadn't been attached to her neck. "Seriously?"

Jennifer's excitement made it somehow real, especially as Shelby's editor never joked. "Seriously! I'm reassigning the rest of your journey across America to Guy Morgan and flying you home first thing Sunday morning so you can get started. If you say yes."

A book. The thought boggled the mind. This was even more of an opportunity than the magazine spreads. "But my car."

Sensing she'd stunned Shelby, Jennifer laughed. "My assistant is already arranging for it to be shipped back to Seattle. That's how confident I am. Timing is everything, which is why we thought to follow your personal narrative with a book debut. One's in March and the other in April. Basically a two-for PR win. We always release a book in spring, and it's you! There's a special addendum to your employment contract to sign, but you can have an attorney look it over. I can assure you the terms are generous and fair."

What did you do the moment all your career dreams came true? Flabbergasted, Shelby stood on the curved floor and stared blankly.

"I never thought I'd see you speechless," Jennifer noted with a laugh. "And you shouldn't worry. It's late September so you'll have to move fast, but I know you can do it."

Shelby snapped into the present. "I'm flattered and, and... I mean, yes. You know the answer's going to be yes. I want to do. Can do it." Sounding overly enthusiastic, Shelby added quickly, "As long as the terms are solid."

"You'll be pleased. I'm so excited for you."

"I'm excited, too." Shelby moved so another group could peer out the window.

"Good. Then it's time to celebrate."

They made their way to the tram boarding and a park ranger directed them into a car. They stopped for dinner in the city's vibrant Central West End, eating outside under lights strung over the patio and then walked off the delicious meal by strolling down Euclid Avenue.

They returned to the inn close to nine. Jennifer retired to her room, and Shelby sat on her bed. She opened the electronic copy of the book contract.

She'd call the family attorney first thing—his office was a few blocks down—but he could review it online. If he told her it was good, she'd tell everyone.

When she returned from preparing for bed, the screensaver on her laptop changed to a slow-moving slideshow. The current display was a photo of her family at the fall festival. A lifetime had passed since the photo had been taken. Something caught her eye and she peered closer—Luke was in the background. Normally she paid better attention to backgrounds, but as she'd somewhat blurred this one to focus on her mom and dad, she hadn't inspected the crowd.

She shut the laptop and climbed under the covers. Race weekend began with tomorrow's glow. Several balloonists were staying at the inn while others were at various motels or the closest campgrounds. She rose and paced, too keyed up and giddy. Eight pages in the magazine and a book! Her hard work and dedication had paid off. All her dreams were coming true.

All but one.

When Shelby woke the next morning, her first thought was she'd slept soundly. The minute her head hit the pillow, she'd fallen into a dreamless sleep. The second thought—she grabbed her phone and opened the local weather forecast, confirming it was going to be a gorgeous weekend. No mystery cold fronts or even the slightest chance of rain. Sunny and cool enough to fly.

She scrambled out of bed and went for her morning run. She'd jogged about a mile when she heard crunching on the trail behind her and heard her name being called. She turned down the music volume and glanced over her shoulder. She knew that voice. Dressed in a wicking T-shirt that clung to abs she'd palmed with abandon and running shorts that hid the part of him that had given such pleasure, Luke ran up behind her and Shelby's mouth dried. He caught up with her and adjusted his stride to hers. "Hi, Luke."

"We ready for tonight?" he asked, as if deliberately keeping his tone casual. But she heard the underlying hint of hurt.

"As ready as we'll ever be."

He easily kept pace beside her. "I think Dad's suspicious. He hasn't said anything, but it's like he senses something's going on."

"Maybe someone in town got wind of it. Ha. Unintentional pun." Shelby laughed off her nervousness.

"Maybe. Our moms know. And we did have to add you as being the pilot. Plus, we were at state. People saw us. They do talk."

"Nothing is secret in this town." Probably not even the fact she'd spent the night with him. Imagine the speculation and gossip had she spent the entire weekend.

They sprinted around a slower runner, Luke

edging somewhat ahead. He slowed again. Shelby's watched beeped, intruding. "My time to turn around. I'm taking my editor into Hermann for lunch. I'll be back in time for setup."

"See you later." Luke jogged ahead instead of turning around with her. She brushed off her disappointment. He made a good running partner—they were in sync in so many other ways, too. But she had a busy morning. Things to do.

She spoke with the lawyer. She accepted the contract over lunch at one of Hermann's riverfront restaurants. Then she and Jennifer toured some of Hermann's historic sites and enjoyed a glass of wine at one of the local wineries. They arrived back in Beaumont by 3:00 p.m. Shelby parked behind the inn. "I've decided not to tell anyone yet. Flying *Playgroup* takes priority. Maybe at the dinner tomorrow night. That might be a good time. I haven't worked it all out."

"I would think you'd be yelling it from the rooftops, but my lips are sealed," her editor promised. "And I can't wait to meet Luke."

Luke, the reason Shelby wanted to wait. He'd be excited about her news, she knew. But telling him before the race seemed wrong, like putting a big distraction in the way or letting an elephant into the room. Tomorrow was their last L&S adventure. She wanted the day to be special. With no baggage from the past or invasions from the future. Just flying and being in the present.

They found Luke waiting for them outside the building that housed his apartment and the art gallery. "He's quite handsome," Jennifer whispered as Luke came into view.

"Shh," Shelby warned, drinking in his attractiveness. He wore blue jeans better than any model. His soft, forest green chambray long-sleeve shirt emphasized his forearms, as he'd rolled up the cuffs to almost his elbow. His eyes appeared fathomless. "Luke, this is my editor. Jennifer, this is Luke."

When Luke shook her editor's red-tipped manicured hand, Shelby swore her editor's cheeks darkened as she blushed. Luke had that way with women. "Anna's already with my mom, and Carl and Lisa will meet us there with *Playgroup*."

"Okay." They drove to the city park, the same one where they'd first tried to fly from the day the lines were tangled. Was that only two weeks ago? Felt so much longer. She certainly wasn't the same person who'd arrived from Iowa, the one who planned to drop into town quickly and drop out just as fast. She was calmer. More centered. More aware of others and more self-assured in who she was. She owed much of that to the change in her relationship with the man next to her. Even if that relationship couldn't go anywhere beyond friendship. Even if the thought of him with anyone else made her taste bile.

Luke drove to the pilot entrance and rolled down the window.

The guy working the gate did a double take. Shelby recognized him as Bill Lewis, someone they'd attended high school with. "Luke!" He handed over their access buttons. "I saw Carl bring in *Playgroup*. Did your dads decide to fly?"

Shelby leaned forward. "Hey, Bill. I'm flying."

He peered in the truck and made a mark on the clipboard. "Good for you. You're checked in. Spot three."

"Oh, this is going to be fun," Jennifer said from the back seat. "Do you know everyone?"

Shelby laughed. "Pretty much. Welcome to life in a small town."

They arrived at their assigned spot. Carl and Lisa were already there, unloading *Playgroup* with Bruce and Kate. "What can I do?" Jennifer asked.

"Come here, I'll show you," Lisa replied, putting Jennifer to work spreading out the fabric.

Luke accompanied Shelby to the pilots' briefing, which was being held under a large, open-air pavilion. Shelby signed in, garnering more shocked glances by those seated at the table.

"Shelby!" The town mayor approached with the race organizer. "I couldn't believe it when I saw your name. And Luke! So excited you're here."

"You wanted the town to have an entry," Luke said amiably. "We couldn't let you down."

They found their seats for the glow briefing, and afterward Shelby and Luke accepted greetings from their fathers' contemporaries as they walked back to *Playgroup*.

Shelby found *Playgroup* laid out and ready to inflate. She made short work of assembling the burners and performing final inspections. She secured the burn schedule inside the basket.

"What's next?" Jennifer asked.

"We hang out and picnic. Visit with others or wander around until it gets dark. Then we inflate and people wander through. There's a show at seven thirty."

"There's a show?" Jennifer asked.

"Yes. It's hard to explain. But envision a wave or a Whack-a-Mole game but with balloons all set to music."

"How intense is this competition?" Jennifer sat in a lawn chair, a plate of cheese and crackers in her lap.

"Not at all. It's more about bragging rights. While ballooning has a competitive, sponsored circuit, our town doesn't take part, something I appreciate. This is far more relaxed and friendly."

Shelby settled into a lawn chair and reached into the picnic basket. Their group chatted until Shelby's watch beeped at the programmed time. "Let's stand her up."

Luke yanked the pull cord to the fan, which started pushing out massive amounts of air. Their crew held the skirt open, and all around them, the noise of fifty balloons being pumped full of air overtook the evening. The additional sound of burners soon joined the fans, and around them, balloons stood tall.

Playgroup tried to fly, and Shelby's crew all leaned on the sides of the basket to hold it down to the ground while Luke and Carl worked to secure the tethers. Across the field, swaying and colorful balloons dotted the night, glowing brightly as the sky darkened.

The festival opened, and onlookers began to wander through. All night Shelby and Luke experienced the joyous surprise of friends, neighbors and former teachers and classmates who came over and, once they saw Shelby and Luke, got excited.

Especially Mrs. James, who bustled up and was positively delighted. "Shelby! Luke! Who would have known you would have taken me so seriously."

"I'm cashing in on those cookies for life," Shelby joked.

Mrs. James gave her a thumbs-up. "You've got them. Whatever flavor you'd like."

"Chocolate-chip. You're lucky I don't live in town or I'd be by every day."

"I'm fine with giving you cookies every day. Thank you for doing this." Mrs. James and her family moved away. The thankfulness continued as other townspeople, including members of the city council, came by and said how delighted they were to see *Playgroup*.

Then it was almost time for the light show.

"Uh-oh," Lisa warned. She rose from her lawn chair and approached the basket, where only the wicker wall separated Luke and Shelby. "Incoming."

Luke's dad, mom and Anna wove their way through the field of balloons. They hadn't noticed *Playgroup* as spot three was on the farthest edge of the field from the entrance.

"Shelby. What are you doing?" The question came over the whoosh of the burners and Shelby jumped. Busy looking in one direction, she hadn't watched her back. She pivoted.

"Hi, Dad." She swallowed the guilt. "Mom."

"What is this?" her dad demanded, a frown on his face.

Shelby made an adjustment to control the burn. "*Playgroup* glowing."

Not pleased with her answer, her dad folded his arms and widened his stance. "I can see my balloon. What's it doing out?"

"Standing up?" she offered, hoping Luke would jump in.

But behind her, he had bigger problems as his parents came into view. "Luke! What the heck?" Mr. Thornburg yelled. He saw Shelby's dad and immediately went on the offensive. "I warned you not to take this balloon out."

Not one to back down, Shelby's dad drew himself up to his full height. "I didn't. And it's not your balloon."

Mr. Thornburg waved his arm. "You didn't have permission. I warned you about taking it out of the storage unit."

"Your balloon? I paid for half. You had no right to lock me out."

Even in the light from the glow, Shelby could see her dad's cheeks puff out indignantly. Her mom moved to put her hand on her husband's arm, but he stepped out of reach.

So much for playing nice, Shelby thought. Luckily most of the town hadn't noticed the drama yet, nor had Jennifer, who was wandering around on her own.

"I heard rumors. But to see it with my own eyes… Take it down," Luke's dad ordered.

"Leave it up," Shelby's father contradicted.

Shelby stood in the basket and gazed at Luke. Did he plan to say something? Or was this all on her? Anna, who'd been standing by her grandmother, ran over to her dad and wrapped her arms around his legs. Luke put a comforting arm over her shoulder.

"Stop it!" Shelby's mom and Luke's mom shouted at the same time. Shocked by the outburst, the men could only stare at their wives, who faced them from where they were standing next to each other. Anna peered out from under Luke's arm.

"This has gone on long enough," Shelby's mom said.

"I agree," Luke's mom added.

"Cynthia," Mr. Thornburg said, his lips thinning.

"Don't *Cynthia* me," Mrs. Thornburg snapped. She stood her ground against her husband, and Shelby almost expected her to poke her finger in his chest. She didn't. "How do you think Luke got the key? Me. I gave it to him."

"He and Shelby are flying and you two are going to deal with it," Shelby's mom added. Laura looked at her husband. "Do you understand?"

Lisa's mouth was wide open, and Luke appeared a tad shocked as well.

Anna's eyes were as round as saucers. "Dad, why are they yelling?"

Shelby spoke up as her watch beeped. "It's part of my photo spread that I fly *Playgroup*. Don't ruin this for me. Or the town."

Around her, burners began to fire, following the preset schedule race organizers had distributed. With the burners flaring, Shelby couldn't hear what was being said. No matter what the men argued about next, Shelby refused to ruin the choreography. She started a full burn, and for the next ten minutes she concentrated on the sequence. The field of balloons glowed in all sorts of formations—a wave, a random pattern, from the outside in—until only one balloon was lit in the center, and then a sequence from inside out until the only the balloons on the edges were lit up. Then just the edges and a bull's-eye. Music blared, and the crowd loved the show. They could watch it from inside the field, or at the edge, where cameras placed on cranes beamed images onto a huge display screen.

Then came the big finale: a full burn and then no

burn. After a brief moment of darkness, the crowd cheered. As cheers grew louder, the balloons flickered back on. Shelby adjusted the burners, making *Playgroup* glow like her peers. By the time the show ended, only Luke and their crew remained. Both groups of parents had left.

"What happened?" she asked Luke.

"I'm not sure. About a minute after the show started, our moms dragged our dads off in opposite directions."

She nibbled on her lower lip. "Are we flying tomorrow?"

"I'm not giving them back their balloon." Luke's hands wrapped around the protective covering surrounding one of the metal bars at each corner of the basket. He leaned closer. "Possession is nine tenths of the law. They'll have to steal it back. Carl and Lisa plan on locking it in their pole barn. Nothing's going to spoil one final L-and-S adventure, right?"

"Right." How many had they had? She'd long ago lost count and sadness filled her that this was it. Her watch beeped again, and one second later, the announcer came over the PA broadcast system to announce the night's event was over and to come back the next day at three.

Festival attendees began to leave and, like the previous weekend, the park's streetlights and pilots' auxiliary lights flickered on as pilots and crew began to deflate their envelopes. "Where's Jennifer?"

"She caught a ride home with your parents." Lisa motioned, and her daughter, Riley, who'd hung out with her friends, came over to help. Once *Playgroup* was stored, Lisa and Carl drove away with the trailer.

Shelby glanced at her watch and nibbled her lip. "I'm almost afraid to go home. Did you see how upset my dad looked?"

"Same as mine. How about we go to the pilots' dinner? Better than cheese and crackers or facing them."

Eating sounded good, but Shelby didn't want what the race organizers were serving. "I'm not in the mood for pizza."

"Pick somewhere else. Anna's at my parents and I'm hungry."

The offer to spend more time with him was tempting. Like the week before he'd left for Europe, a sense of impending loss had settled in. Tomorrow they'd be surrounded with family and friends at the pilots' postrace party. Minus flying, this was their last alone time. She wanted to spend it with him.

Her phone beeped with a text message. Sorry to cut out, Jennifer had written. Loved it. We'll talk in the morning.

Fate had removed the final obstacle. Part of her thought to run from her fears. Part of her thought to throw her arms around him and tell him to take her home and love her one last time.

"How about we go to LaBelle's?"

It was the stand-alone restaurant operated by La-Belle's Dairy, which had been their second-favorite place to eat. Arriving, they found the decor unchanged—same chrome chairs with black cushions and backs. The tabletops had chrome edges and legs, and the tops were black-and-white checkered.

The place was packed, but they managed to snag a booth in the back. Shelby scooted onto the black vinyl bench. The teenage waitress came by but Shelby set aside the menu. She always ordered the same thing here: a cheeseburger, onion rings and a chocolate shake, and tonight, that's what she craved. Luke opted for a chicken sandwich, fries and a cola.

"The canvases I ordered for you should arrive Monday," Shelby told him. "There was a delay."

"You never told me what they are."

"It's a surprise." She'd picked out two of her favorites and two newer pictures from the fall festival.

"You always had good surprises." Strong fingers that had caressed her body unwrapped the paper napkin and removed it from the flatware.

Nostalgia. That's all these intense pangs tugging at her heartstrings were. "You were easy to surprise. You scared easy, too."

"Not anymore. I had to lose the habit when I had Anna. Now I'm the best bug killer you ever saw."

"What about snakes? You still like Indiana Jones?"

He shuddered. "You picked it up and dangled it."

"It was a harmless garter snake in your mom's

garden and he was in our way. Someone had to move him to safety."

"Trust me, I've instructed Anna on Missouri snakes, but I'm not getting close to them."

"Wimp," Shelby teased. "I did a photo series about this village in India that ignores the country's ban on snake charming. The practice has been banned for forty years, but the Bedia claim it's culture. They defang the Cobras."

"I read that article. Great photos." His compliment warmed her, and she watched as he removed the ketchup from the condiment holder and set the bottle in the middle of the table. He caught her eye and smiled. "Have I ever told you how much you amaze and impress me? All the places you've been and the things you've seen. Our imaginary pirate adventures seem so tame now. Lame, even."

She laughed. "Hey, don't knock those. They were great times. They gave me my zest for life. When I'm working, I'm focused on the job, not the adventure. It's so second nature for me to have a camera in my hand, I feel naked without it. Even sitting here, I see things I can photograph."

"Good thing it's safely locked in the truck. This way I have your full attention. Unless you want me to grab it?"

"No. And you always have my attention." He always would. When she left this time, a part of her would remain behind. She'd also carry with her the longing to touch him. To be with him. She'd learned something else by being home these two weeks. She didn't relax. She was constantly moving or doing something. If she kept moving, the silence didn't creep in.

She sipped her water. "You asked me what I do for fun. The answer is I don't know what to do when I stop traveling."

He reached for her hand. "You sit in Labelle's with me and drink a milkshake. We can hang out anytime."

He made the answer seem so simple and how she wished it was. The waitress approached and set down Luke's soda and Shelby's chocolate shake. The dairy served its shakes and sodas in clear, double-walled, rippled goblets. Shelby picked up the long-handled spoon and lifted out the cherry. She held it out to Luke. When he took the stem out of his mouth, he'd tied it into a bow.

"Still don't know how you do that." Shelby stirred the whipped cream into her shake.

"My one special but odd talent that serves absolutely no purpose but to make a great party trick." He set the twisted stem on the tabletop. "So do you fear anything?"

Losing you. The thought burst forth and took root, and Shelby thrust it aside with a frantic sense of desperation. "Scorpions. I saw someone whose leg swelled up after a sting. He's fine but..." She shuddered. "Those for sure."

"Yeah, spiders, snakes and scorpions. No thank you. I'll pass."

His friendly tone kept the melancholy from taking hold. She remained grateful he kept the conversation light, and they chatted like old friends. The waitress brought their food and set their plates in front of them.

Then, without even asking permission or realizing they did it, they each reached forward. Shelby took a handful of Luke's fries. He took four of her eight onion rings. Shelby squeezed out ketchup onto her plate. Their fingers touched as she passed Luke the bottle before he asked. He lifted the top off his bun and added ketchup. Then he took the lettuce and tomato from the side of her plate and stacked it on his burger. He passed over his pickles, and Shelby added them to her stacked cheeseburger. She pointed to his chin after he'd taken a few bites.

"What?" Luke wiped his chin with a napkin. Tried again.

Shelby leaned over the table and dabbed her napkin on his chin. "There."

She leaned back, suddenly highly aware of the innocence yet intimacy of the gesture. Luke's eyes had darkened. "Thanks."

"Welcome." Rattled by the easy way she'd slipped into his personal space, as if she belonged there, she grabbed her glass and drew up the last vestiges of chocolate shake. The metal straw rattled against the empty goblet. She rested both hands on her stomach. "This is exactly what I needed."

"Me, too. I don't get out often unless it's Anna and my parents."

More proof he was home and hearth and she was not. "You think our dads are still mad at us?"

"Maybe a little. It's more a case of their pride being dented, which they deserve. Trust me, I've got a plan to fix it. I'll let you know if it works."

"Okay." She put her hands on her stomach. "It's nice your mom watches Anna all the time."

"My mom loves it. Maren's parents are happy in Florida. We FaceTime with them. We'll try to see them soon."

"You didn't date after Maren?"

"No. Why would I?" He didn't say anything else, but Shelby heard his thoughts. She was the reason he didn't date. And for selfish reasons, she simply couldn't tell him that he had to get over her, especially as it would be a long time before she got over him.

Their waitress approached. "Dessert?"

"No, I'm stuffed," Shelby replied. "You?"

"I'm good," Luke added.

Their waitress removed the check from her apron and put it on the table. Seeing the amount before Luke picked up the slip of paper, Shelby reached into her camera bag and pushed the bills into the middle of the table. "This is on me."

He hesitated as if to argue, but gave in. "Okay. Thanks. Now what?"

Shelby twisted her paper napkin. "I want to go home with you. But I don't want to be the one who comes into town and we hook up."

He frowned. "Is that what you think we did? Is that why you freaked out last Saturday?"

"I don't know. Maybe." She rose. Felt Luke behind her as she led the way to the exit. While he didn't put a hand on her lower back and stayed a good foot behind her, her awareness intensified. Silly hormones. Pheromones. Biology. Anthropology. Sociology.

Whatever it was, she thought as they walked to the truck and climbed in, after she left Sunday morning, she had to get over all of these turbulent emotions. Maybe they needed one more night. Prove last Friday was a fluke. An aberration. That the sex wasn't that good. No, she couldn't do that. It had been perfect.

"You're not a hookup," Luke said as he started the engine.

"Then what is this? I like kissing you. I didn't want to say no last weekend. But I'm afraid of having regrets. Like what about your next girlfriend? Our families are friends. What happens when you bring her home for Christmas and she has to run into the ex you slept with? Before we were kids. Our teen behavior is excusable. But when we're adults? I can't fall into bed with you every time I come home, no matter how much I want to. Being with you is not like eating brisket at Miller's."

"I would hope not," Luke said. His headlights cut through the night. "I don't want to be an itch you need to scratch."

"You're not. But we can't be more. Even if I want you like I do."

Uncertainty, doubt and longing settled around her like the misty halos around the lampposts they were passing. He parked behind his building and Shelby climbed out. The moment of truth had arrived. He waited for her to follow him upstairs.

"I want to kiss you. I want to stay with you to-night." She stepped closer to Luke. She absorbed his scent and rested her head on his strong chest. She tilted her chin for him to kiss her until her toes tingled. But he didn't because he knew there was more. She sighed. "I feel like I'm messing with both our heads."

"All we are guaranteed is this moment." Luke held her fingers lightly in his as they stood there in the soft glow cast from the dusk-to-dawn light overhead. "But you have to be sure and you're not. I'm deciding for us. As much as I want you in my arms and in my bed, you're right. It's not just sex for me. There are deep feelings involved on my end and you're leaving. And I don't want you to feel guilty."

He knew her so well. Walking away tonight would

be one of the hardest things she'd ever have to do, but leaving Sunday would be harder if she didn't. Yet her heart wanted him to make love to her one more time. Just so she could remember it forever.

Warring emotions threatened to overwhelm, and somehow she managed to step away, severing their connection. "Who knows, maybe we'll win tomorrow. Good night."

He let her go and softly said, "Good night."

The air seemed to chill after she walked away, and she wove between the buildings and stepped out into the historic street. A hazy thickness wrapped around the tall, wrought-iron streetlamps, the still night air crisp and clean. A waning gibbous moon shone, creating long shadows on the cobblestones. The street contained a strange stillness and an odd silence. A night thick with atmosphere, as if the Woman in White had walked the street and brought finality with her.

Even a Main Street Halloween complete with a full moon didn't feel this spooky. Shelby quickened her steps, as if trying to outrun the ghosts of her past. She sprinted up the steps to the front porch and pressed the code to open the front door. A few lamps blazed in the living room and the parlor. Taking a calming breath, Shelby secured the door behind her. Then she crept up the main stairs as quiet as the still night and tiptoed down the hallway past the guest bedrooms. She reached the end of the hall and the locked door to the back stairs. As she unlocked it, her camera bag slipped and bumped the wall. Shelby stilled it, but no guests opened their doors. She slid through.

Reaching the third floor, Shelby went into her room, flicked on the light and closed her door. She set down the camera bag. She'd already dragged her larger suitcase out of the closet and placed it on a luggage rack. Clean clothes already packed waited inside, ready to be secured. She'd pack the smaller carry-on tomorrow night, after the race. A freight service had already picked up her car.

Sunday she'd be on a plane, wheels up for Seattle and the next adventure—a book deal. She'd throw off these invisible chains wrapping around her heart. Stop eating all the home cooking and behaving like mythical lotus flowers urged her to linger. Shelby drew the cover to her chin. Thirty hours until she unpaused and dove back into her life.

Chapter Ten

Sometimes Missouri weather got it right, and as if knowing Shelby could use some positive vibes, race day turned out to be one of the state's ideal two hundred and five sunny days. Shelby rose early, went for a long run in the high-fifties temps, and returned in time to shower and help her mom serve the guests blueberry pancakes with maple syrup and powdered sugar.

By the time Shelby carried the remaining plates into the kitchen, her mom had most of the dishes done. "How mad is Dad?" Shelby asked. "I feel terrible I put you in the middle."

"You didn't put me in the middle. I did. And he's fine. Deep down, he's proud of you. I'm sure he would have said something if he hadn't been so shocked."

"Luke and I foolishly thought they'd be happy and put aside their differences after they saw what we were doing."

Her mom started the dishwasher. "It was a good wake-up call for them. They realized they can be replaced, and they needed that. If it's not by you and Luke, the town has a year to sponsor someone else, local boys be damned. They should be worried."

"It won't be me. I'm one and done. I wasn't planning on flying when I first arrived. Not at first, even after Luke asked me. But then Jennifer mentioned assigning me the feature spreads, and I couldn't pass up the career move. I'm about to get even busier." Shelby had decided to share her book-deal news, but she wanted to tell her parents together.

"Your career matters to you. You're a trailblazer, especially for young girls."

"Thanks. As I'm writing a personal story, my ego demands I try to win. Then flying became even more. I loved being in the air with Luke. You know what it's like up there. I needed it. The peace. The calm. The pure joy of flying." *Of being with someone who meant the world to me.*

No, she couldn't say the L word.

"Sounds like these weeks have been good for you."

"They have. But I still want Dad and Mr. Thornburg to be friends. We hoped that maybe if our dads saw that we could fly together, especially given mine and Luke's turbulent history, that maybe they'd realize how silly their feud is. I've seen Luke's plans for the building and some of the construction. Caldwell's is going to be brilliantly redone and Luke's ideas are exactly what the town needs. I wish I'd had access to a darkroom space like the one he's building. Anna's going to get to have the best of both worlds just down the street."

"Talk to your dad. Tell him this. Make him understand."

"That's my plan. Is he here?"

"No. He disappeared early this morning. He didn't tell me where he was going."

"I'll catch him later. I'm trying to have a strike-free day."

"I'm sure you will. Now go check on your guest."

Shelby found Jennifer out on the front porch, on her phone. Jennifer held up a finger, finished her conversation and smiled at Shelby. "Good morning. Ready?"

"Can't wait. As long as it's calmer than last night," Shelby said.

"I can't believe I missed the drama. Your dad didn't say a word on the drive home. You really weren't kidding, were you? How are you? Are you okay? No aftereffects?"

Only waking up and wondering if she'd made the biggest mistake of her life walking away from Luke. Goodbyes were always hard, but she'd been saying them her whole life. She could manage this one. "I'm fine. Look at today. I'm flying later and the weather is perfect. Once I get up there, the world literally drops away."

"And you'll be with Luke."

"We're friends." Shelby heard the lie, but thankfully Jennifer didn't.

Instead, she watched people pass by on the sidewalk. "I can see why you like it here. This street is frozen in time and an authentic piece of Americana. It's going to make a fabulous feature."

"Things move slower but we do have high-speed internet."

"Thank goodness. Even though it's Saturday morning, I've got proofs to review. There's always work to do. I'll catch you later."

Jennifer went inside and Shelby remained on the porch. Merchants wouldn't open their shops until 11:00 a.m., but the restaurants served breakfast and brunch. She checked her phone. The temps would top out around seventy today. A good sign.

Shelby heard a door slam and saw Anna skipping down the sidewalk. She saw Shelby and stopped. "Hey, Shelby," she called. "Whatcha doing?"

"Hi, Anna. I'm drinking my coffee." Shelby held up her mug.

"Stay there. I'll be right back." Anna waved and went inside. A few minutes later, Anna came racing out the front door and tearing up the porch steps. "I made you this," she said. She thrust a folded white piece of paper at Shelby. "It's a card."

"I see that." On the front, using crayons, Anna had drawn a pink-and-yellow hot-air balloon. The brown basket held two people—one male and one female. "That's Dad and you." Anna pointed to the names she'd printed next to each stick figure. Luke was wearing blue jeans and a green shirt while Shelby had on some polka-dot pants and a red top. "Grandma told me how to spell your name. That's *Playgroup*. My orange broke, so I used pink instead."

"It's perfect." Shelby's eyes watered and she fought back the tears. She opened the card and read aloud. "'Thank you Shelby for teaching me photos. I will miss you. Love Anna.'"

Some of the words didn't fit the margins and ran onto the next line, but the letters were all correct. "Grandma helped me spell everything."

"Thank you. It's wonderful. I'll treasure this forever." Shelby pressed it to her heart and gave Anna a huge hug.

Anna wiggled free. "Can we take more pictures? Do you have time?"

Shelby wiped her eyes and nodded. "Yes. Let me go grab my camera and we'll go."

Anna followed Shelby inside and upstairs. "I like your room. It's pretty. Ooh. A music box."

Shelby took it down and let Anna hold it. Anna opened the lid carefully and the music tinkled out.

"It's 'Edelweiss,'" Shelby told her. "Your dad was with me when I bought it."

"My dad likes you," Anna announced. "Are you going to be his girlfriend? You should be. You make him happy."

Anna's words made Shelby's heart pound. Being with Luke made her happy, too. "No, I'm leaving tomorrow. I'll be too far away to be your dad's girlfriend."

Saying those words hurt.

"Oh." Anna absorbed Shelby's words. "I have a boyfriend."

"You do? Really?" Shelby wondered if Luke knew this.

Carrying the music box carefully, Anna wandered around the room looking at things. "Yep. He's in Ohio. His name is Jackson. He said he'll always be my boyfriend even if I moved."

A twinge of jealousy flared. Life was clearly so much simpler and easier in kindergarten. "Well, it doesn't work the same when you're a grown-up. But your dad and I are friends, and I'll see you every time I come into town."

"Okay." Anna handed Shelby back the music box. Shelby put the Swiss chalet on the mantel, still open and playing. Eager to take pictures, Anna bounced toward the door. To keep the card from being damaged, Shelby set it in the side pocket of the open suitcase.

Shelby's throat tightened and, as if to stop her emotions, she shut the lid. Joy and sadness mixed and she swallowed the lump in her throat as the enormity of leaving hit her. While she'd experienced the tenderness and love of a small child, no one had ever truly wormed her way under Shelby's defenses. This wasn't a strike one, Shelby told herself. Tonight after the race would be no different from any other time an assignment ended. But as they headed out the door, the last notes of "Edelweiss" ended and the waterwheel stopped. As if sensing Shelby's sudden hesitation, Anna came back and grabbed Shelby's hand. Anna gave a little tug. "Come on, Shelby. Let's go."

They arrived about five minutes apart, the way Luke planned it. John Bien arrived at Caldwell's first. He stepped through the unlocked front door, entering the work-in-progress main space. The framing was done and putting up drywall had started.

"Wow. This is fantastic" were Shelby's father's first words.

"Thanks." Luke swelled with pride. Mr. Bien was like a second dad to him, so the compliments meant a great deal. "I'm excited. The project is on track. Maybe even a day or two ahead. We open the first weekend in November."

"After you texted me this morning, I logged into city database and went back over all your plans and permits in greater detail. I never would have thought of bringing this exact idea to Main Street. Or of asking Shelby to fly *Playgroup*."

"I'm a problem solver. It seemed like a good solution. Maybe it took moving away and living somewhere else to realize exactly what I missed. This is my home. It's where I'm raising Anna."

"Beaumont is a special place," John agreed.

"I've always considered you like family so I'm going to be honest. This fight between you and my dad, over this?" Luke gestured to the room. "Did Shelby tell you what happened between us?"

Mr. Bien nodded. "My wife filled me in."

"For twelve years, our pride got in the way. The first real test of our friendship and we fell apart. I lost one of the best things in my life and I've regretted it ever since."

"She is pretty special."

"If we can work through it, surely you and my dad can figure this out."

The door opened, and Luke's dad walked in. He stopped short as he saw John Bien. "Why is he here?"

"Because I invited him. Because you two need to talk. I'm tired of all the drama." Luke had spent the last twelve years in an unrecognized funk. No more.

"Look around you," he told his dad. "Look at what this place is becoming. I never envisioned owning a bar. But a makerspace?" Luke gestured at the blueprints. "This will be a community hub. If all goes well and the business plan works, then who knows?

Maybe we buy the place next door and expand. Besides tech and photography and pottery, we could offer glass blowing, painting and fibers."

Certain he had both men's attention, Luke continued. "There's classroom space for lectures. I could offer free ones on things to discuss with your attorney. Or how to set up a simple will. The bottom line is this—you two need to work out your issues. It took me and Shelby twelve years to figure out what went wrong and to start over." He prayed it wouldn't take twelve years to see her again.

"Listen, son—" his dad began.

"No, you listen," Luke interrupted. "If Shelby and I can be friends again, you two can figure it out. I'm not having to tiptoe around next time I see her because you two can't be civil. Arguing over whose pride was hurt more seems a poor excuse to lose a friendship and makes you both terrible role models for my daughter."

Silence fell and Luke's dad shifted from foot to foot. "Well, when you put it that way, we sound—"

"Like stubborn old fools who just got our egos handed to us," John said, finishing for him. "Deservedly so."

"Very much so." Luke's dad appeared sheepish.

Luke picked up a drafting pencil. Set it back down. "I wish I was as close to some of the guys I went to high school with as you two are. And college? I've lost touch with most of them. What you two have is special. You're brothers. Maybe not actual DNA blood, but certainly in all other senses of the word. Don't you know how much we all envy you? Why the whole town has been so upset by this dumb feud? Because when you two aren't fighting, you are a living example of what a lifetime friendship looks like. And who doesn't aspire to have that?"

"When did our kids get so smart?" Luke's dad asked.

"I don't know," John answered. "I guess we are a pair of old fools."

"Definitely agree with that," Luke's dad said gruffly. "Truce?"

"Truce." The two men shook hands. "And our making up will make our wives happy."

"I have missed our foursome for golf," Luke's dad added. "Maybe we can play eighteen holes next weekend."

"I'll get it set it up," John said.

Luke sensed the shift in the atmosphere. Neither man was going to apologize for his behavior, but then again, perhaps that was their way. They'd clearly closed the door on their fight by agreeing to play golf. They'd move forward and pick up like before, as if what had happened between them was nothing but a brief misunderstanding. Luke shook his head at the irony. People really were so fascinating.

"How about I show you both around?" he suggested.

"That'd be great, son. I didn't want to pry so I gave you your space, but I've been so curious."

"I'd love to see it, too," John added.

"Where you're standing in our flex space," Luke told them. "We can use this for small receptions and discussion groups. We kept the bar for both historical aesthetics and practical purposes like serving food and drink for receptions. Note how I'm finishing everything to blend the past and the present."

Luke moved them through the space, explaining his vision. The process took a good hour. Both men asked questions and listened to his answers. Being skilled businessmen themselves, they posed hypotheticals and offered suggestions. Grateful for their advice, Luke made notes on a scratch pad.

His dad had thought of some issues Luke might have and offered fixes. Mr. Bien offered ideas that would make the space work more productively and efficiently. By the time they finished, Luke felt more invigorated than overwhelmed. "This has been great. I'd love to continue to pick your brains."

"How about lunch this week?" John suggested. He looked at Mike. "Can you get away?"

"Absolutely." His dad clasped his hand on Luke's shoulder. "Thanks for doing this, son. Took the younger generation to kick us in the rear. And good job in here. I'm proud of you." He glanced at his friend. "We're proud of you."

"And glad you moved back to Beaumont," John added. "You're really part of Main Street now."

Coming from the two living men he admired most, their words of praise and encouragement meant so much. Even though Luke had a lot to learn, he felt equal to them in business and as a man. "Thanks."

"Now if we could get Shelby home," John said. He gazed at Luke hopefully.

Those worlds acted on Luke like a downer. "Doubtful. She's meant for bigger things than this town. She's meant to fly."

Luke meant fly metaphorically, like beyond Beaumont, but her dad took him literally and checked his watch. "Not too long from now, either. Mike, what are you doing this afternoon?"

Mike shrugged. "Well, not flying. Someone took my—our—balloon."

Luke grinned. "Yeah, me, and because of it, you both get to watch Shelby soar. Having you there will mean the world to her. You know she's writing about your feud as part of her narrative? What better ending for her story could there be than for you two to make up and crew for the next generation?"

His dad exaggerated a sigh. "I know when we're beaten."

John laughed. "Well, apple pie is better than humble pie any day, and I found another one sitting on the kitchen counter this morning. Come on. Lunch is on me."

Luke watched his dad and Mr. Bien leave through the front door. He turned off the lights and exited. He was locking the front door when he heard a voice. "Was that my dad and yours walking down the street?" Shelby called.

"Hi, Dad!" Anna walked over carefully as she had Shelby's camera balanced on her neck.

"Yeah. The feud's over. They'll be part of our crew today."

Shelby's expressions changed from disbelief to surprise to delight. "Seriously? You did it! Wow. How?"

"Some tough talk and an appeal to their better sides." Luke didn't share the details of how he'd mentioned her. "Figured if we were going to have one more adventure, everyone needed to be there."

He might have imagined it, but for a moment he swore Shelby's lips quivered. Then she flung herself into his arms. "Thank you."

Holding her felt so right. She nestled in his arms like she'd been born to fit there. He would have kissed her and held her forever if Anna hadn't pulled on his shirttail. "Dad, picture."

"Okay." He wrapped his arm around Shelby's waist and stood hip-to-hip as Anna adjusted the lens like Shelby had taught her.

"Cheese!" Anna called. She made her shots and lowered the camera.

Shelby pointed to something behind him. "We

have a few more things to shoot and only a few more minutes to finish. I'll meet you soon?"

"Yeah." The time would allow him to regroup. His heart remained in his throat as she and Anna headed up the street. The two chatted easily, and when Anna's shoe snagged between one of the cobblestones, Shelby was right there to help her—Shelby's main concern was Anna and not the expensive camera dangling from Anna's neck. As if sensing him, Shelby turned, smiled and gave him a friendly wave.

Seeing Shelby's smile was like receiving a punch to his gut—how could he let her go?

He loved her.

Part of him had never stopped loving her.

They'd known each other forever. She'd always been his better half. At thirty, he was older, wiser and mature enough to know the rapport they shared and these emotions he felt didn't exist anywhere else. He aspired to achieve the love his parents had. What the Biens had. Twelve years later, he loved the woman she'd become.

He wanted Shelby now and forever.

But when you loved someone, you put her needs first. Luke had been selfish once and not trusted her. He wouldn't make that mistake again. He put the keys in his jeans pockets and strode down the street. He couldn't tell her he loved her, or that he wished she'd stay.

It wouldn't be fair to ask her to choose between

her career and him. They'd fly *Playgroup*. He'd make sure her last night in town was light and fun. No matter how much his heart hurt. Then he'd do the right thing—say goodbye and let her go spread her wings and soar.

Shelby thought the upbeat, friendly atmosphere at the city park served as a good sign. All the people she cared about surrounded her as they pulled *Playgroup* out of the trailer. It was like old times, and she'd hugged her parents and Mr. and Mrs. Thornburg upon their arrival. Having her dad and Mike there also allowed her time to take photographs. As pilots who knew *Playgroup* intimately, they offered better directions to the crew than she could have. Her dad helped her assemble the burners. Mrs. Thornburg wrapped the protective coverings over the poles and basket edges. Mr. Thornburg double-checked the lines and the envelope.

As at the state race, the public remained behind safety tape. This time, however, the weather wouldn't change. No front full of surprise rain approached; the entire Midwest sat under a blessed bubble of high pressure. Shelby and Luke attended the pilots' briefing, which was relaxed and informative.

They returned to *Playgroup*, whose envelope waited to be inflated. They sat in lawn chairs, talking among themselves, until way off in the field, a bright red balloon with three yellow-and-green stripes stood up. The hare balloon was ready, and it lifted into the air to the sound of huge cheers. The hare got a fifteen-minute head start, and then all around, hound balloons began to inflate and take off as race officials cleared each team to fly.

Shelby checked for buoyancy, and nodded at Luke, who was standing next to her. Then she looked at her dad, who gave her a thumbs-up. "All we need is the signal," she said.

"Step back," Luke told Anna, who moved away from the basket to stand by her grandmother and Jennifer. Everyone else continued to lean on *Playgroup*, holding the basket down and keeping it from skipping, and once Shelby received the official sign to launch, she checked the instruments and yelled, "Okay. We're good."

"You got this," her dad said, giving her outstretched gloved hand a fist bump. "Go get 'em."

Then he let go of the basket, as did everyone else, and Shelby fired the burners to send *Playgroup* skyward. *Playgroup* rose smoothly and joined the balloon-filled sky—her first time piloting in this situation. But Shelby and Luke worked well together and she felt confident in her abilities, and in *Playgroup* and the instrumentation. Shelby could spot the hare balloon far off to the southeast, as a long twenty-foot "leg" hung outside the balloon to clearly mark it.

While she'd never done this part, her dad and Mr. Thornburg had explained what happened next.

Once the hare landed, its chase crew would bring out another twenty-foot section and place it down to create a giant X. Never losing sight of the temperature inside the envelope, but not having to keep her hands on the burner the entire time, she lifted her camera and took a few shots. She pointed her lens up, aiming into the envelope. She captured the shadow of the balloon against the trees. She took a picture of Luke as he operated the GPS, topography and tracking programs. Far below them, their chase vehicle followed.

After checking the instruments, she burned more fuel to add heat into the trapped air, increasing their altitude. The sun would set at six forty, so having drawn an earlier spot and taken off around four forty, they had approximately two more hours of flight time. Behind them, the sky was dotted with balloons all traveling the same direction with the goal of dropping a beanbag filled with birdseed closest to the X, which was what won the race.

Since this was her last flight of the year—maybe for years to come—she wanted to stay in the air as long as possible. Down below she could see cars pulled over on the shoulder or in parking lots. People craned their heads out windows or stood outside their vehicles, where it was safe to do so, and watched over their heads as fifty hot air balloons of all designs and colors filled the sky over Beaumont.

The balloons drifted east toward the Missouri

River, and depending on their altitudes, Shelby and all other pilots worked burners or vents in the crowns in order to be in the correct altitude range required to cross over the water below. The hare balloon drifted ahead, into the next county, its leg dangling in a visible challenge. Shelby got a great photo of it.

As they flew on, she and Luke talked about all sorts of things: other balloonists, what they saw on the ground and what photos Shelby was taking. They purposely avoided anything dealing with them personally. She thought about telling him about her book, but didn't because she still hadn't told her parents.

They were flying into a more populated area and since they'd been flying for over an hour, Shelby knew the hare would choose a landing spot soon. *Playgroup* had been one of the first fifteen balloons launched, which meant thirty-five pilots followed behind.

"They're going down," Luke said, pointing at the hare. He consulted the GPS. "They're going to be landing in that school parking lot."

The hare descended and the moment the balloon came into range, its crew was out of their truck and ready. A crew member grabbed the dropline and help the hare land. Once down, the crew got to work. They deflated and moved the balloon out of the way. They set up the target and established a safety perimeter to keep onlookers out of the way of the bags soon to drop out of the sky.

Traveling with the wind meant all balloons moved at similar speeds, with any slight variations depending on the air currents at the various altitudes. The higher they went, the faster the air moved. However, sometimes moving into a different altitude meant the wind at that height changed directions. *Playgroup* had the latest in wireless flight-pack instrumentation, for which Shelby was grateful. She made some mental calculations of flight speed and time needed for their descent over the target. She watched as the balloons in front of them began dropping their bags.

"We're getting close. You ready?" she asked.

Luke held up the beanbag attached to a twenty-five-foot tail containing their names. "Ready and willing. Or do you want to throw?"

"No. We're equal partners in this. I fly, you toss."

He grinned. "Just say when. I'm leaving that up to you."

"Will do." Shelby began to vent the crown. Five seconds later, *Playgroup* descended and the big X on the ground grew closer. "Now?" Luke shifted his gaze from her face to over the basket edge and then back.

"Not yet." Shelby leaned over in an attempt to see the target better. She expelled more air. They'd dropped to a thousand feet, but they weren't close. She let out more air, dropping even lower. She sent up a silent prayer. If she'd calculated everything right, the target should be almost directly below. She adjusted the vents and closed them. "Now!"

Leaning over, Luke dropped the beanbag, and Shelby fired the burners to lift them back up. She looked behind them, watching as the twenty-five-foot trail spiraled downward until it became too small to be seen. "Well, that's that."

They both looked behind them, back toward the target and the remaining field of balloons that filled the sky. "I say the bag landed close," Luke said.

"Hopefully. It'd be fun to win."

"Is this where you say if not, it's the effort that counts?"

Shelby grinned. "You know me and my competitive streak. Start looking for a landing spot. I guess that's one good thing about being an early launch. We get to be one of the first ones at dinner. Or stop by the inn and clean up."

Luke moved closer. "Or we could fly some more. It's nice up here. I can see why my dad loves it. And your dad. Let's fly away. Never go back. You, me and the sky."

He was half-serious, Shelby realized. "I know what you mean. This has been great. Even though I'm literally concentrating on flying, I'm relaxed. And I never relax."

She closed her eyes and lifted her face toward the sun for a moment. Sighed and opened them. "But we'd run out of fuel eventually, and you'd miss Anna. We should be near the community college. That should have some decent fields or parking lots we can use."

Luke checked the map and pointed to a spot in the distance. "You'll have your pick." He sent a text to their chase vehicle and read the return message. "They can see us. I'm letting them know the plan."

The moment bittersweet, Shelby tried to remain positive. "Great. I'm sad to end the adventure, but it's time to set her down."

Shelby pulled the crown line. Soon she had the college beneath her, and she set them down on the baseball field. *Playgroup* bounced once as the deflated envelope dragged, but the basket remained upright.

Within seconds, two cars' worth of their family and friends were there, giving hugs and helping to pack away the balloon.

"You looked so good up there," Shelby's dad said, and she noted a bit of wetness in his eyes as he gave her a hug.

"That was incredible," Jennifer said, giving Shelby a hug as well. "I can't wait to see what you write."

"You'll have to go up some other time," Shelby told her.

"Definitely."

"You're always welcome," Shelby's mom told Jennifer. "And the night's not over. Dinner and awards to follow."

"I took pictures of you coming down," Anna said,

not to be left out. Shelby had loaned Anna a DSLR camera and a kit lens.

"I can't wait to see your photos," Luke told his daughter. He lifted her up, gave her a big hug and set her down again.

A low flying balloon went by overhead and landed in parking lot close to them. "Time to go," Shelby's dad said. "Let's free up this space for the other teams to land."

Shelby rode with her parents and Jennifer while Luke drove his parents, Anna and *Playgroup*. Because they had some time before the dinner started, they stopped by the inn and Shelby changed into fresh jeans and a light sweater.

The pilots' dinner took place at Beaumont Country Club, a public golf course and banquet center. By the time the Bien family arrived, the parking lot was partially filled with cars and trucks, some with trailers attached. "Over here," Luke's mom called, and they went to join them. Anna was home with Riley.

"Date night!" Lisa announced happily. She lifted her wineglass in salute to Shelby. "Thanks for flying. Tonight is always one of the highlights of my year."

Bruce and Kate arrived, and eleven people wedged around a table for ten. The meal began with a starter of tomato bisque, a choice of roast beef or lemon-glazed chicken, or both if you asked nicely. Sides included white-wine linguine or mashed potatoes, green beans, iceberg salad and rolls. The open bar served wine, beer and cocktails, and Shelby decided on a celebratory French 75, which was a combination of gin, champagne, lemon juice and simple syrup.

When everyone held a beverage, Shelby's dad raised his glass. "To Shelby and Luke. For showing us old dogs we could learn some new tricks."

"Who are you calling old?" Luke's dad joked. Then everyone raised their glasses and chorused, "Shelby and Luke!"

Shelby's cheeks heated as she touched her glass to others. Underneath the table, Luke gave her hand a quick squeeze for support. She hated being the center of attention, and when her editor dinged her fork on her water goblet, Shelby's stomach dropped. She frowned and shook her head at Jennifer. Tried to catch her gaze.

"Speaking of toasting Shelby, now that it's official, let me tell you how wonderful her work is and what *Global Outdoors* has in store for her."

Oh, no. Shelby had planned to tell everyone, then she simply hadn't found the perfect time. Besides, her mom would make a big fuss. Want to celebrate. And as excited as she was, Shelby kept waiting for the other shoe to drop. That, and the man seated next to her had consumed her thoughts. "Jennifer, really…" Shelby began.

"Shelby, I know you're bashful, but you did say after the race." Jennifer kept her glass up. "I've enjoyed visiting Beaumont this week and putting faces with names. I can see where Shelby gets her grit and work ethic. Ever since I hired her right out of college, she's impressed me with her drive and her ambition, and her willingness to always sign on to the latest adventure. Which is why I'm delighted to tell you that each year *Global Outdoors* publishes two coffee-table books and *Around the Globe* by Shelby Bien will be our April debut."

"Shelby!" Her mom threw her hands up and then around Shelby. "I'm so proud of you! Dreams do come true!"

"Thanks. Yes, it's exciting." Shelby enjoyed their congratulations, but she wished Jennifer hadn't blurted out the news here.

Next to her, Luke raised his longneck in a silent toast, and Shelby had to acknowledge that not all of her dreams had come true. He leaned over. "Congrats. It's what you've worked so hard to achieve."

But at what price? "Thanks. It's a great opportunity. I'm sorry I didn't tell you. I meant to."

"I get it. You were busy. Don't worry, I'll be sure to buy one. You'll have to autograph it."

"Of course. It would be an honor." She could sense their separation as Luke turned back to his meal, and as sadness threatened, Shelby tried to enjoy the present. The mood lightened somewhat by dessert. Servers at a dessert bar distributed oversize plates of gooey butter cake, chocolate and carrot cakes, and a selection of bite-sized donuts. "You get the gooey butter and I'll get the chocolate. Then we can split them," Shelby suggested.

They returned to their table to find the others had gone. Jennifer, citing their early flight and work matters, had taken an Uber ten minutes ago. Bruce and Kate were at the bar with Lisa and Carl, and both sets of their parents were talking to their friends. Their parents wore huge smiles on their faces.

Shelby motioned towards them. "That's good to see. Feels like all's okay with the world. This is good chocolate cake."

Discussing dessert—like talking about the weather. Safe. Noncommittal.

"So's this." Luke took bite of gooey butter cake. "Sorry your editor had to leave."

Shelby scooped up some of the frosting. "She's a workaholic. If she hadn't stayed at the inn, I wouldn't believe she actually sleeps. You should see the Thanksgiving dinner she and her husband hold. I don't know how he keeps up. She's always going and going."

"Sounds like someone else I know."

Shelby shook her head. "Not these last two weeks. Not as much, anyway. It's been nice to slow down for once. When I get back, I'm on a tight schedule for putting the book together. Can you believe it? A book with my name on it, filled with my pictures."

She reached her fork forward and dug into the iced edge of Luke's gooey butter cake. She wrapped her lips around the fork tines. "Yum. This is good, too. I'm hoping I don't mess things up. Maybe that's why I didn't say anything once I learned about the book deal Thursday. It doesn't feel real."

"You'll be fine. It'll be like yearbook. Mrs. Benedict will be thrilled."

"I heard she retired. I'll have to send her one."

He reached his fork into her plate for another morsel. "I think it's almost announcement time." They made quick work of their desserts and by the time they'd finished, everyone had returned to their tables.

"I'm nervous," Shelby said.

"Whatever happens, you made the town proud," Luke said.

The festival organizer spoke first. He thanked all the sponsors, and if they had representatives in the room, those people stood to be acknowledged by claps and cheers. Then the town mayor added thanks, including mentioning the pilot of the hare balloon. He took out the folded piece of paper and smacked it against his palm. The crowd laughed. "The moment you've all been waiting for. Here we go."

The room stilled with anticipation as he unfolded the paper and gave it a quick skim. "Third place is Dan Smith, of Ames, Iowa, flying *Currents* for State University. Altitude of eleven hundred feet and sixty feet from the target center."

The table of Dan Smith and friends erupted in

cheers and Dan went up to receive his trophy and thank his sponsor.

The mayor came back to the microphone. "Next is second place, going to Oskar Lutz, of New Rochelle, Missouri, flying *Big Dog* for Mel's Hot Dogs at nine hundred twenty feet and thirty feet from the target center."

As Oskar's table cheered, Shelby leaned back, discouraged. "Those guys are good and got a lot closer. There's no way we placed."

Her mom patted Shelby's arm. "We're proud of you no matter what the results are."

"We tried," she whispered, ready to clap for the winner.

"And in first place," the mayor paused. "Drumroll?"

The crowd began to bang their fingertips against the table in a rapid staccato. At their table, Luke reached for her hand and held it tight. After a short moment of noise, the mayor's voice grew excited. "And the winner is, and, no, it's not a fix, Shelby Bien of Beaumont, flying *Playgroup* for the town of Beaumont, at eight hundred and sixty feet and thirty feet from the target center."

The room burst into cheers. Stunned, Shelby pulled her hand from Luke's. Her mom leaned over and hugged her.

"Get up there," her dad urged.

Sensing her indecision, Luke jumped to his feet

and pulled Shelby to hers. He gave her a slight push. "Go."

"No." She hated these things. Didn't know what to say. "You dropped the bag."

"Up here, Shelby," the mayor called.

She turned to Luke. For someone who'd bungee-jumped into gorges, she didn't have these skills. "Come with me."

"Okay." Luke laced his fingers through hers. With Luke's hand a comforting weight, Shelby allowed him to lead her to the front. She smiled for a photo op with the mayor and then passed the trophy to Luke. Stepped to the microphone and stared into the mass of people waiting for her to speak.

"Hi." She heard her voice echo through the speakers. Luke nodded his encouragement. "I've been watching my dad and Mike Thornburg fly for years. I know how much *Playgroup* means to this town, so when I heard it might be grounded and Luke asked me to fly her, I'll admit, at first I didn't think I could do it. But Luke believed in me. And he dropped the beanbag, so thank you to Luke for being my partner." She paused briefly at the word as if she'd stumbled over it. "You've always been my partner in adventures and believed in me when others didn't. Words can't express what that means. And thank you to my crew, and to the town for sponsoring the balloon and this wonderful event that brings us here tonight. And finally, thanks and love to my parents, and to the Thornburgs, who are my second parents. Thank you for always having my back."

"Always!" her dad shouted across the space. Shelby stepped back and the crowd erupted in cheers. The mayor concluded the ceremony and the DJ struck up the first song, a fast, late-seventies disco classic drawing most of the older crowd out on the dance floor within seconds. The event photographer drew Shelby and the other winners aside for photos. When it was her turn, she and Luke, and their families, and Bruce and Kate, smiled for a group photo. Then Shelby had to take one by herself for the hometown paper, and then one with the other two pilots.

Fifteen minutes of photos later, and then another ten minutes of pilots who kept stopping them and offering congratulations, she and Luke finished their official duties and returned to their table. Shelby put the trophy on the center of the table and thumped into her chair. Lights and other objects reflected from the trophy's shiny metal surface. "I can't believe we won."

Luke's knee pressed hers and she welcomed the contact. "Believe it. You did it."

"*We* did it." She pointed to the eighteen-inch, gold-plated hot-air balloon with the year and *Playgroup*'s name etched on it above the first-place designation. "I know your dad and mine have a fifty-fifty sharing rule for any trophy, but I'm never home. Put that in Caldwell's. If it's in my apartment, it's just collecting dust." And she wasn't sure if she wanted the reminder of him.

Luke's brow creased. "Are you sure?"

A lump formed in her throat. "Yes. Put it somewhere people can enjoy it. We won this for the town."

"We did." Luke brushed a loose piece of hair out of her face and she longed to press her cheek into his palm. "It was fun. I liked having this adventure with you."

"Me, too." The wave of sadness she'd been trying to hold back hit her full force. Magazine feature! Book! Trophy! She should be over-the-moon happy with how things were going.

But sitting this close to Luke, with her hands almost on top of his, all she could think about was how much she'd miss him. And how, for once, she didn't want to leave Beaumont—didn't want to leave him. With a soft smile, he reached forward, taking a loose strand of hair and twirling it around his finger before setting it behind her ear in an intimate movement.

Shelby faced a hard truth and one she couldn't run from. She adored him. She yearned for his touch. She— *No! Don't even think it.* The truth was, the more she stayed, the more her heart would break. Sudden urgency to flee consumed her and she glanced around to find her parents. They were on the dance floor.

A conga line started, and partiers began to dance and weave their way through the tables. "Hey, you two," Lisa shouted at them. She motioned for them to join her before putting her hand back on her husband's shoulder. "Get yourselves out here."

Shelby stood, but she didn't move to follow Lisa. Instead, she gave Luke an apologetic smile. "I should go. I've got an early flight. I'll get an Uber. You stay and enjoy the party."

Sensing her mood change, Luke rose. "I'll take you. My parents can ride home with yours."

His mom came to the table to get a sip of her iced water. "I'm driving Shelby home," Luke told her. "Can you and Dad ride with the Biens?"

"Absolutely." Mrs. Thornburg embraced Shelby, holding her tight. "You take care, dear. Have a good flight and don't be a stranger."

"I'll try," Shelby promised, but the words rang hollow. She and Luke left the party and stepped into the quieter, darkened parking lot. He opened the passenger door, and even though he didn't need to, helped her into the truck. She enjoyed his brief touch far too much, and once inside, held her own hand as if trying to preserve the tingles for when the nights would be long and lonely.

He must have felt the same, as before he started the car, he gave a sharp exhale and said, "I hate this."

She hated it, too. He turned to face her. "I hate that you're leaving. I hate that we're only friends. I swore I wouldn't say anything to ruin that friendship, but I can't let you go without letting you know how I feel."

"Luke…" she began. *Please, no, don't make this harder than it already is.*

He leaned closer. "Twelve years ago, my New Year's wish was to love you forever. I know it's only been two weeks. But it's like those years we've been apart and mad don't matter. Exploring the feelings I have for you has told me one thing. This isn't puppy love or a high-school infatuation. I know the difference. Making love to you sealed the deal. It's why I understood why we shouldn't repeat it. We'd crossed a line. The intimacy mattered. It held a mirror to my feelings."

"Luke." Her lips quivered as she tried to contain all her tumultuous emotions. "Please don't. This is already hard enough."

"I've waited twelve years to tell you the truth. Twelve to make myself worthy of you." He pressed his palm against her cheek and she leaned into it, trying to memorize the texture. "You're the only one I want, Shelby. It's always been you."

How long had she waited to hear those words! He was her dream man. The one she'd always loved and desired. Her other half.

His passionate voice washed over her. "I can't let you go back to Seattle thinking I don't care about you. I adore you beyond measure. We understand each other. We eat each other's cake. We fit. I know what's it's like to have someone love you, and not be able to love them in the way they deserve. I thought

I gave a hundred percent, but Maren was right. Deep down, as much as I denied it, I held part of me back. There was a part of me I couldn't give her because I'd already given it to you."

"Luke." Her heart tore into a million pieces, but as he held her cheek softly in his palm, she refused to move and end the moment. *What would she do if he asked her to stay?*

Kiss me. Ask me to stay. She willed the words as his lips came closer.

"There was a hole in my life Maren should have been able to fill, but she couldn't. It remained because you are the only one who could fill it. You are my soul mate. It's always been you."

Each word pierced her, not because they hurt— they did—but because she felt exactly the same. She wanted him. She cared for him so much. And she had to leave. Unless… She waited, sensing there was more. She pressed her forehead against his.

"It's okay, Shelby. I'm not asking you to stay. I know you can't. Your life isn't here, and to ask you to stay and be with me is selfish, especially when I wouldn't do the same and move to Seattle with you. I won't uproot Anna again. But maybe I am selfish, because I couldn't let you leave without knowing how much I care for you and tell you how much you mean to me. So much that I'm not going to stand in your way. Your life is out there. Go get it. Live your dreams. Grab that brass ring. I'll be cheering you on."

Once he'd been her dream. Once he'd been her everything. Shelby's heart splintered even more. How could he be such a wonderful man as to accept the fact he had to let her go? And then to give her what she wanted?

Even if she wasn't sure she wanted it now?

He straightened. "You shouldn't have to choose between me and your dreams, because you deserve all the success coming your way. Tomorrow, when you board the plane, don't look back. Don't worry about me or tether yourself to any guilt. Don't do that. Instead, go grab the adventure. You're ready to solo. You always have been. Now there's nothing holding you back. I can't wait to see where you go next."

She wanted to go into his arms, Shelby thought as he started the engine. But she'd missed her chance. She knew Luke couldn't fight for Shelby because Anna had to be his priority. But suddenly she felt lonelier than ever before. Although, she reminded herself this was what she wanted. What she'd told him these past two weeks. She wanted her career. Stood on the precipice of all her career goals.

It was no comfort.

Luke remained her dream man, but her career beckoned, including the accolades to follow, things she'd worked so hard to achieve, including being a role model to little girls like Anna by reaching the top of a male-dominated field. Walking away now seemed foolish. Perhaps it had been good coming home, if only to put the past to rest. Luke would move on. So would she. He drove her to the back parking lot of the inn, taking the spot where her car had been. He met her beside the passenger door as she stepped out.

He appeared sheepish. "Sorry to have dropped that bombshell on you. But I needed you to know. Made for an awkwardly quiet ride home."

She couldn't risk putting her hand on his arm. If she touched him, she might wrap her arms around him and never let go. "I'm glad we cleared the air. I wish…"

He leaned as if to kiss her on the cheek, and she stepped back and shook her head. No matter how much this hurt, it was better to make a clean break. If he kissed her, she'd never leave.

"Stop. Whatever you do, don't wish things could have been different. Maybe in some alternative universe we were together from high school on, but in that one you wouldn't have Anna. She's a great kid. And in that universe, I wouldn't have traveled. And we wouldn't have won tonight." She held out her hand. "Friends."

"The best."

Despite her resolution to keep some distance, Shelby pulled him to her for one last hug. She held him tight, imprinting him on her brain and drinking in his aura and his delicious scent. She noted the tightness and heaviness of his arms. The hint of sage and sandalwood. The thump of his heartbeat. The way she fit him. She memorized everything, planning to draw on the memory forever. One of her top-ten best nights ever. Even if terribly bittersweet. Even if full of heartbreak.

He drew back and she closed her eyes when he planted a soft kiss on her forehead and a gentle one on her lips. Then he broke the connection, turned behind him and reached into the vehicle.

"Don't forget this." Luke handed her the camera Anna had borrowed. "Thank you for teaching her."

"Anytime. Good night." Shelby walked the path to the back door, hoping with every step he'd call her back. That wouldn't be fair, she knew, but pain still stabbed her when he didn't. He'd said he wouldn't, and he'd meant it. She kept her chin high as she passed their bench and refused to cry as she pulled open the screen porch door. She forced her feet to climb the backstairs. She'd left her camera bag at home when she'd changed clothes, and she put the camera Anna had borrowed back into its case and zipped it closed.

Her big suitcase was packed and closed, with the clothes she'd wear tomorrow on the plane already set on top of the open carry-on. Shelby changed into her pajamas. Today's outfit and the pajamas would stay here, for when she returned for the holidays. Christmas, Shelby promised herself. She hadn't been home for the traditional Main Street Christmas in forever. She'd attempt it this year. Try to make sure nothing came up.

Something always came up.

Shelby stared out her bedroom window and across the way to Luke's childhood bedroom. The window remained dark, but as if the ghost of her past life visited, Shelby could easily picture Luke across the way, waving at her or sending her messages in Morse code. Was there a time when she couldn't remember him being there? Her childhood companion and her best friend.

Her coconspirator. Her first crush and kiss. Her first lover.

Her first heartbreak.

Her dream man. Her other half. Always.

Unsettled, she climbed into bed. Bright and early the next morning, she kissed her parents goodbye before climbing into the car Jennifer had ordered. They sat in the airline lounge preflight, and an hour later she held out her phone as the gate agent scanned her boarding pass for her first-class seat, a perk she'd received for earning over a million miles a lifetime ago. Jennifer scanned her pass and, after stowing her luggage, dropped into the aisle seat to Shelby's left.

"You seem sad," Jennifer observed once the flight attendant dropped off coffee for Shelby.

"Just tired." Shelby clicked her seat belt. "Sun's not even up in Seattle."

Jennifer held a sleep mask, ready to put it on once the safety demonstration ended. "Which is why I'm going to use some of this time to get some extra shut-eye. Tomorrow we hit the ground running. Meetings at nine a.m., and then…"

Shelby couldn't concentrate. She half listened as Jennifer outlined the schedule. The flight attendants performed the safety demonstration, and the plane pulled away from the gate.

The plane taxied to the runway and, cleared to depart, picked up speed and launched into the sky with a rumble of its huge, diesel engines. Shelby stared out the oval window. The wind direction meant the plane had to bank and turn to fly west. Down below, off in the distance, she could see the Missouri River, and beyond that, a speck that was Beaumont.

Then the speck was gone, left behind as the plane worked its way to thirty-two thousand feet. Leaning back, Shelby adjusted her earbuds to soft music and closed her eyes. *I'll get over him*, she told herself. *I have to.* The world waited.

Chapter Eleven

"What do you think of this one?" Jennifer asked, flipping to a new slide.

"Better than the last," Shelby said. She studied the projection screen located in the magazine's smaller conference room. She and Jennifer were finalizing photographs they'd chosen for Shelby's book, this time to approve the page designs. Once Shelby accepted the layouts, the copy she'd written to accompany each photo would replace the fill text that acted as a placeholder. A copy editor worked on those files, editing to house style.

Shelby should have been excited. The layouts looked gorgeous. The book would be beautiful, and a preview of the cover... Shelby had been speechless, it was so stunning.

She picked up her coffee cup and realized the contents had grown cold. She'd been back in Seattle for the past month, working twelve hours a day. She'd dusted her fake ficus and filled her refrigerator with essentials. Halloween was in two days. Even though she didn't expect anyone to knock on her apartment door to trick-or-treat, she'd purchased a small bag of candy, anyway. Just in case. After all, she'd never been in her apartment on Halloween before. She imagined Luke would take a costumed Anna up and down Main Street, where the merchants stayed until seven to host a trick-or-treat event.

As for Thanksgiving? She'd been invited to Jennifer's annual holiday gathering, which promised turkey and all the trimmings. Shelby had attended before. Jennifer invited an eclectic group of people; it was the one time a year Shelby saw most of them.

"I like the third layout the best," Shelby told her.

"That's the one I like, too. Number three, it is. Now that this section is settled, how's the narrative for the magazine coming? You have a week if you're to have time for revisions. I'm starting to get concerned. You still haven't picked out the dominant four images or sent me a draft."

"I'm almost done. I'm tweaking the copy." In actuality, Shelby had written one hundred and two words in total. Every time she sat at her laptop to work on the narrative or to sort through the photos, she simply couldn't do it. There were too many memories in the way and she'd been unable to break through the funk.

For the first time, she'd stalled. When she'd moved to Seattle for college, she'd been so angry. Desire to prove herself and put Luke behind her had partially fueled her passion. She'd thrown herself into her work and the constant escape it offered.

Her rage had dissipated years ago, but she'd continued the hard work and the thrill of seeing more and more of her work published. Now she stood on the brink of triumph, but instead of joy, she felt deflated and listless. As if the memories of her two weeks with Luke were too hard to deal with. Or maybe her melancholy came from the gray skies of Seattle. Except for college, she'd never stayed in town for this long a stretch.

"Stop tweaking," Jennifer said. "Your book copy and captions were excellent. Thanks for pushing that text out so quickly and meeting your deadline two days early. Have you talked to him?"

Shelby straightened. "What?"

"Now I have your attention. You've been somewhere else the last few minutes. Have you talked to him?"

Shelby shook her head. She'd gone to the salon, washed out the blue and trimmed her hair, which she wore down, trying on a different style to encourage a different mood. "Luke? No. My parents, yes. They're fine. They're going to his grand opening. I told you about his makerspace."

Her parents had sent her a snail-mail, official invitation for the first Saturday in November, which was three days after Halloween. She'd held the card stock and thumbed it many times. In addition to the date and time of the event, the invitation contained multiple pictures of the space, one of them an image of the wall where her photo canvases hung. Shelby pointed to the screen before Jennifer asked if Shelby planned to attend the grand opening. "Don't we have more pages to go through?"

"Yes, we have the next section to work through." Jennifer pressed a button and the slide changed. "Do you like this one?"

The colors chosen clashed with the photos. "Not feeling it," Shelby said. "Next."

Hours later, Shelby sat in her apartment. The cursor of her laptop sat flashing under the last word she'd typed. Her microwave dinged and she pulled out a chicken Parmesan meal. She peeled back the plastic film and stirred the sauce and noodles together. Cut into the chicken and sighed. Forced herself to take a bite—it could never come close to the flavor of her mom's cooking.

Two weeks at home had spoiled her. The first week she'd been back in Seattle, she'd ordered carryout food. To save her budget, she'd stocked up on frozen food, mostly prepackaged meals.

Dinner consumed, Shelby rinsed out the plastic tray and set it inside the recycling bin. She filled a glass with ice water and returned to her laptop. Might as well bite the bullet and finish the magazine spreads, she thought. She couldn't put off the inevitable, and she really wanted these spreads. Career photographers learned to become emotionally detached, especially those who photographed trauma and war zones. If they could do it, she could go through the images. But there was Luke. *Playgroup.* Her family. Beaumont.

She pushed through, trying to assess and judge each photo on its technical composition and visual interest. Methodically, she assigned the photo one star if she thought she might send the image to her editor. Then she sorted to see just the one-star photos and repeated the process, this time removing the star. By the time she was done, she had finalized the last of the photos for Jennifer.

Shelby stood, her legs itching to move. She'd run earlier. However, a quick walk around the neighborhood couldn't hurt; it might help clear her head. She could shoot a few photos of the skyline. Then she'd come back and tackle the text.

Deciding that leaving the apartment might help get her creative juices flowing, Shelby retrieved her camera bag. Since she'd mostly been choosing images and writing captions for the book, she hadn't used any of her cameras since she'd returned. Probably the main reason she was in this funk.

She reached for her preferred camera, and then, deciding not to bother with swapping out lenses, Shelby grabbed the camera she'd loaned Anna. She opened the card slot to put in her memory card in, and frowned as she discovered a card already in the slot. She closed the door and turned on the LCD display to review the photos. Immediately, she realized these were Anna's shots from race day. Shelby began to thumb through them, sending each photo to the cloud. Then she reached the last few photos. The ones Anna had taken before the race, when she and Shelby had run in to Luke leaving Caldwell's.

Anna had held down the shutter button, meaning she'd taken multiple shots in rapid-fire sequence. In the first few, Shelby and Luke were looking directly at the camera. In the final few, he'd turned his head. While she still faced the camera, he faced her. She zoomed in on his face.

She touched the image with her forefinger, as if trying to feel the texture of his cheek. She knew almost every one of his expressions. But she'd never seen this one before…although she knew it well. She'd seen the same loving expression on her father's face whenever he held her mom close. She'd seen the same warmth on Mr. Thornburg's face whenever he held his wife's hand. She'd seen a similar look anytime either man watched his wife, as if she was the only woman in the world. And all over the world, Shelby had photographed couples wearing the same expression.

Abandoning the idea of going for a walk, Shelby tossed a bag of popcorn in the microwave. Once it had popped, she took out the bag and let the steam escape. She put a few pieces into her mouth and decided she wasn't hungry. No one made popcorn like Main Street Pops!, the candy and popcorn shop in Beaumont. Same for Auntie Jayne's cookies. Same for the brisket at Miller's Grill.

Seattle, for all its charms, wasn't home. Home was where everyone knew her name. Where her photo hung on the wall in city hall for winning a hot-air-balloon race. Where the man she loved hung her pictures on his wall and put the trophy they'd won together out for proud display.

She'd lived in Seattle for twelve years, but she'd never planted roots. She hadn't joined any groups. While she had a Washington State driver's license and was a registered voter, she hadn't bothered to get a library card. She hadn't hung pictures on the beige walls of her apartment, which remained as bare as the day she moved in. She hardly wore the few clothing items hanging in her closet. Her closet's primary function was to store her multiple suitcases.

Speaking of suitcases, she really should send out her laundry. She went into her bedroom and reached for her larger suitcase, the one she'd checked through on the plane ride back from Beaumont. She'd gotten home and immediately shoved it next to another piece of luggage she hadn't unpacked from a previous trip. Time to sort and unpack, which would give her something to do. After she finished, she swore she'd write her narrative.

As if trying to exorcise her demons, she unzipped the case she'd had in Beaumont and flipped open the lid. She removed three tops and put them on hangers. Then her fingers hovered before they went to the pocket on the side. She slowly unzipped it and gently removed the folded paper. She smiled wistfully and ran her forefinger over the pink-and-yellow crayoned balloon on the front side.

She touched the male figure in the slightly lopsided basket. Anna had drawn Luke and Shelby with bright red lips and wide smiles and linked hands. Closing her eyes, Shelby pressed the card to her heart. She remembered perfectly Luke's hand in hers, and how warmth fused their fingers together. She liked how whenever she had his fingers laced in hers, she felt as if she could conquer the world. Her heart longed to show her love, and she wanted to kiss his lips and feel the texture of his five-o'clock shadow. The walls of the apartment closed in and she dropped the card back into the suitcase. Closed the lid.

Not with a bang but a whimper. T.S. Eliot. *My life closed twice... Parting is all we know of heaven, and all we need of hell.* Emily Dickinson. Tears threatened. Shelby couldn't do this anymore. A walk, she reminded herself. She was going on a walk. She headed for the door.

Luke gazed at the substantial crowd flowing into the newly opened Main Street Makerspace. The well-received soft opening had been a good harbinger of how tonight's grand opening would perform, and Luke wasn't disappointed. He wandered through the venue, noting how well his employees greeted guests and explained the various areas to young and old. His mother worked the membership table, and memberships had already exceeded expectations. His sister and Riley worked in the child-care area, where Anna assisted by reading picture books to toddlers. The last time he'd seen Anna, she'd told him she was having a great time.

He wished he was. He'd put everything into this renovation and business, and its success was everything he hoped for, but something was missing. Shelby. Throwing himself into the rehab and installations had helped, but not once had his work eased his heartbreak. He remained restless, his fingers eager to call her, but he'd known he shouldn't. He had to let her go. She deserved to be happy and successful.

"You did good," his father said. Together they looked down into the main room from the glass wall on the second floor. "This is all everyone in town can talk about."

"As long as the momentum holds." Luke pulled his hand from the front pocket of his jeans. He was also wearing a white oxford button-down—sans tie—and a casual dark blue sport coat.

"It will," his father predicted with confidence. He gave Luke a congratulatory clap on the back. "You've got a great staff in place and good infrastructure. You've got a good head on your shoulders, and I'll advise if needed. But I doubt you will. You did it, son. You got everything you wanted."

Not quite, Luke thought. He didn't have his soul mate. But he plastered a smile on his face and began to mingle. Many attendees had questions, and he answered those and gave personalized tours.

He'd scheduled the event to end at 9:00 p.m., but because he didn't lock the doors, the crowds remained until ten. Finally, around a quarter past, guests began leaving.

"I'll man the door," his dad said as Luke came down from the second floor. "Go push any stragglers in this direction so you can lock up."

"Will do." Luke headed toward the wide hallway leading to the darkroom, where Shelby's photos hung. He'd loved the canvases the moment he'd opened them. Two were landscapes—one from Everest and one from Paris. The others were Main Street. One was the entire street, the lines of the buildings and the street all leading to a point in the center where the cobblestones ended at the horizon. The last one was of his family's booth, with Luke standing outside it, holding Anna's hand. Anna was looking up at him, and he at her.

In her note, Shelby had told him to feel free to sell any of the canvases to start a scholarship fund, but Luke couldn't bear to part with them. Minus the photo he had of him, Anna and Shelby standing on the train, he had nothing else from September. He'd funded the scholarships himself.

"Luke? I'm going to take Anna home," his mom called. "I'll go up and get her."

"Okay. I'll turn the lights out down here and then we'll lock up and walk home."

He entered the hallway with the photos. A figure wearing a dress and black heels was standing near the end, studying the photo of Luke and Anna. "Hi there. We're closing and…"

He stopped. As soon as he'd started speaking, he'd recognized her stance. Her hair might be in a knot and she might be in a little black sleeveless dress, but he knew her. "Shelby."

She turned and gave him a shy smile. "Hey." She pointed at the canvas. "These came out really well."

He approached slowly, as if uncertain she was real. "I've gotten a lot of compliments on them."

"I'm glad." She touched the canvas and smiled at him again.

Luke took a deep breath as his heart clenched in agony. Not enough time had passed since he'd seen her last. His gaze roved over her. He studied the line of her jaw, the smoothness of her neck, the fullness of her lips and the brightness of her hazel eyes. She'd looped a sweater over her arm. She was so beautiful, both inside and out.

"I walked through the space," she told him. "It's wonderful. I'm so impressed and happy for you."

"Thanks. I'm glad you could make it. I didn't think you were coming."

She seemed hesitant. "You know me. Any excuse to travel."

He could only stare, afraid she was a ghost, and if he looked away, she'd be gone. "How's the book coming?"

"My part's done and it's in production. I'm working on writing the magazine copy now."

"The balloon-race spreads? On Beaumont." Flummoxed, he remained rooted a few feet away. Her surprise appearance had him off-kilter. She appeared a vision.

She smiled and it hit him in the solar plexus. "Yes. It took me all week. I sent in a rough draft before I got on the plane."

He shoved his hands into his pockets. "That's good."

She sighed. "Actually, it's not. I don't have an ending and I've hit writer's block. Beaumont inspired me, so I came home to finish it. I dropped my stuff at the inn and came straight here."

She gestured to her clothes. "Wasn't sure how formal this was, but it's better to be overdressed than under, right?"

She gave a high-pitched laugh, which was odd because Shelby was never scared. While she might not like being the center of attention, even back in high school she'd been brave and daring. "I knew this was important and I realized I couldn't miss your moment. And selfishly I figured you could help me out. I'm stuck. I need your help."

A twinge of disappointment tempered his initial excitement. That's why she was here. Her magazine article. He couldn't let his heart break again, but he'd help her. Of course he would. That's what friends did. He deliberately made his next words casual. "How long are you staying? Couple of days?"

"It depends."

She closed the space between them and a burst of hope flared. "On what?"

Shelby held his gaze. "On you."

As Luke's face registered her words, Shelby reached her hand forward and pressed her palm against his cheek. She knew she'd hurt him, and if he'd let her, she'd spend the rest of her life making it up to him. She'd spent the last five days writing and making decisions. How their story ended remained unwritten. But she knew what she wanted to say. "I don't deserve your forgiveness. But I hope you will offer it and let me come home."

"What do you mean? You'll have to spell it out."

His gaze never wavered as it locked on to hers, and Shelby tried not to nibble her lower lip. She'd jumped out of airplanes. Crawled on her belly through caves. Those hadn't frightened her as much as getting through the next few minutes.

She inhaled in a failed attempt to steady her fraught nerves. She reached out, taking his hands from his pockets and lacing her fingers through his. "I've lived my life out of a suitcase for twelve years. I've run from my roots. From you. From how I feel about you."

His hesitant expression didn't change. "Which is how? Explain so I don't misunderstand something this important."

She hadn't expected him to go easy on her. She wouldn't have deserved it, anyway. She'd been the one to walk away, to choose to leave him and his love behind. The first time had been accidental. A teenage misunderstanding on both their parts.

This time she'd prioritized the wrong things, hurting both of them again. She'd stomped on his heart, been a fool not to see what was right in front of her. She wanted this do-over. She'd fight for the tiniest sliver of hope and never let go.

"I've spent so long running away. I didn't see what I had when I stopped. The way I feel about you is the same way I hope you still feel about me. Like there's a part of me missing when I'm not with you. There's a hole only you can fill by being in my life. You're my soul mate, you and only you. It's always been you. I told all of this to my editor first thing today, when she asked me why I was so miserable. I also told her I couldn't work there anymore."

Luke's eyes widened and his grip tightened. "You quit? You love your job! I can't let you quit. I won't let you. Not for me."

She shook her head and reassured him. "No, I didn't quit. But I can't live in Seattle anymore. It's a great city, but it's not home. I live in a lonely apartment where I don't know my neighbors. I don't even have clothes hanging in my closet. Jennifer told me to go, so I grabbed my bag and booked a flight. I was so nervous I forgot to tell my parents I was coming."

"They know. We have an audience." Luke gently turned her toward the main room. Her parents and his were all standing at the end of the hallway, watching them. Anna leaned back against her grandmother, her eyes round as saucers.

Shelby gave them a small wave and returned her attention to Luke. "Anyway, I arranged my schedule with Jennifer so I can work from here. I may have to fly back to Seattle every so often, and I'm going to take you with me whenever I travel somewhere exciting, but I'm tired of being a lonely wanderer with no roots. Being with you makes me happier than anywhere else I've been. You're my home."

"I am, huh?"

He smiled and joy flitted around edges of her soul. She could feel the love he had for her. It washed over her like gentle wind lifting *Playgroup.* "Yes. You. Always you. Ask me again."

He cupped her cheek. "Shelby Bien, how long are you staying?"

Her heart pounded so hard and fast, she worried it might burst. Tears of joy ran down her cheeks, probably ruining the makeup she'd applied especially for this. She put her hand on his cheek and leaned close. "I love you. If you'll have me, I'm staying forever."

She stared at him, waiting on tenterhooks. But then she felt it, as if a warm aura of pure joy entered the room. Time paused, encircling them as if they were the only two on the planet. Luke's smile widened with an all-consuming love—the kind that nurtures, envelops and grows—and Shelby knew everything would be okay.

Luke swept his lips down, capturing hers. His kiss wiped the past away and ushered in their present. He pulled back for a minute, and she immediately missed his touch. "I love you, too. A forever L-and-S adventure sounds perfect."

He kissed her again, his mouth on hers until Shelby felt Anna wrap her arms around Shelby's waist. Shelby loosened her arms to draw Anna into the circle as their parents approached to congratulate them.

Home, Shelby thought as, around her, everyone

began talking. The greatest adventures still to come would start right here in Luke's arms, because traveling the globe had taught her one thing. Home wasn't a place—it was where her heart was happy and content.

As Luke kissed her again, her joy overflowed.

Epilogue

Luke and Shelby married the following fall, on a perfect October day, one not too hot, windy or cloudy, in the city's outdoor garden. Shelby walked down a white runner toward Luke, who was waiting in his tuxedo. She passed friends and family—most of the town was attending the nuptials. She held Luke's hands in hers as they recited their vows. The moment the minister told Luke he could kiss the bride, Shelby's husband kissed her thoroughly and passionately, much to Shelby's immense delight. Kissing him would never get old. The kiss also earned the applause of all who witnessed it.

Luke was her husband. She liked the way those words sounded, and she couldn't stop stealing gazes at him as they walked back down the aisle. It was proof childhood dreams really do come true, even if those dreams had taken a few laps around the globe first.

The past year had seen so many changes. Shelby's first book signing had occurred on Main Street, and family, friends and almost the entire town had attended, helping her book sell out—even now, the bookstore kept having to order more copies. Her feature in the March issue of *Global Outdoors* had been well-received, especially with the happy ending that told her readers all about how she'd chosen to return home to her true love. Jennifer had told her that discussion and impressions on the magazine's social media had outdone anything before at the publication. The town loved the spread— it had seen a huge increase in tourism.

Jennifer and her husband had flown in for the wedding, and they tossed birdseed on the newlyweds as Shelby and Luke passed by.

Working from Beaumont had turned out better than Shelby could have imagined. She'd traveled to Seattle a few times, but for a girl who'd run through passports like water, staying stateside no longer felt like a trap. She'd taken both Luke and Anna and their parents with her on her one trip out of the country in July—they'd all spent two weeks on a safari in Kenya. Shelby's next magazine feature was all about that family adventure, and Anna would even get her first professional photo credit.

Beaumont was home, and when one of the smaller, historic houses on South Main Street had gone on the market, they'd bought and renovated it for their main residence. Luke could walk to work—his Main Street Makerspace had not only met its business plans and expectations, but the place was also so popular he was expanding into the building next door. Hobby crafters found a place to play and find joy, and serious crafters developed the professionalism they needed to sell their wares in Main Street shops. Luke and Shelby's dads had placed second in the town's hot-air-balloon race, and Luke and Shelby had taken fourth at state, with Luke as an official copilot after finally finishing his pilot's license and certificate. They'd danced the night away afterward.

Anna loved first grade and was teaching her best friend Megan photography. Last Christmas, Shelby had gifted Anna her first camera, and they'd spent the holiday photographing winter in Rocky Mountain National Park. And simply enjoying being a family.

Over the past year, though, the best thing had been spending time with Luke and Anna. Shelby loved them and the forever life they were building together.

"Are we ready, Mrs. Thornburg?" Her arm still linked with Luke's, they'd reached the end of the white runner. Behind them, their guests began to rise.

She smiled. You could say she'd been born for this. "More than ready."

Arm in arm, Shelby and Luke walked out into the center of the field, her shorter wedding dress designed specifically for what came next. Even Mother

Nature cooperated—while they'd always planned on a short flight before the evening reception, today's wind would carry them directly to the reception site, Jamestown Vineyards, one of the area's family owned wineries. They climbed into the basket and performed their final prep.

"I love you," Luke said, kissing her before reaching for the line his dad handed him.

"I love right you back," Shelby said, reaching for the controls.

Then, as their guests cheered, Shelby let *Playgroup* rise into the clear blue sky, taking them on their first married adventure.

* * * * *

Check out these other great second chance romances, available now from Harlequin Special Edition:

The Valentine's Do-Over
By Michelle Lindo-Rice

Their Sweet Coastal Reunion
By Kaylie Newell

The Bookstore's Secret
By Makenna Lee

COMING NEXT MONTH FROM

H HARLEQUIN®
SPECIAL EDITION™

#2965 FOR THE RANCHER'S BABY
Men of the West • by Stella Bagwell
Maggie Malone traveled to Stone Creek Ranch to celebrate her best friend's wedding—not fall in love herself! But ranch foreman Cordell Hollister is too charming and handsome to resist! When their fling ends with a pregnancy, will a marriage of convenience be enough for the besotted bride-to-be?

#2966 HOMETOWN REUNION
Bravo Family Ties • by Christine Rimmer
Sixteen years ago, Hunter Bartley left town to seek fame and fortune. Now the TV star is back, eager to reconnect with the woman he left behind...and the love he could never forget. But can JoBeth Bravo trust love a second time when she won't leave and he can never stay?

#2967 WINNING HER FORTUNE
The Fortunes of Texas: Hitting the Jackpot • by Heatherly Bell
Alana Searle's plan for one last hurrah before her secret pregnancy is exposed has gone awry! Her winning bachelor-auction date is *not* with one of the straitlaced Maloney brothers but with bad boy Cooper Fortune Maloney himself. What if her unexpected valentine is daddy material after all?

#2968 THE LAWMAN'S SURPRISE
Top Dog Dude Ranch • by Catherine Mann
Charlotte Pace is already overwhelmed with her massive landscaping job and caring for her teenage brother. Having Sheriff Declan Winslow's baby is just *too* much! But Declan isn't ready to let the stubborn, independent beauty forget their fling...nor the future they could have together.

#2969 SECOND TAKE AT LOVE
Small Town Secrets • by Nina Crespo
Widow Myles Alexander wants to renovate and sell his late wife's farmhouse—not be the subject of a Hollywood documentary. But down-to-earth director Holland Ainsley evokes long-buried feelings, and soon he questions everything he thought love could be. Until drama follows her to town, threatening to ruin everything...

#2970 THE BEST MAN'S PROBLEM
The Navarros • by Sera Taíno
Rafael Navarro thrives on routines and control. Until his sister recruits him to help best man Etienne Galois with her upcoming nuptials. Spontaneous and adventurous, Etienne seems custom-made to trigger Rafi's annoyance...and attraction. Can he face his surfacing feelings before their wedding partnership ends in disaster?

HSECNM0123

HARLEQUIN
PLUS

Try the best multimedia subscription service for romance readers like you!

Read, Watch and Play.

Experience the easiest way to get the romance content you crave.

Start your **FREE TRIAL** at
www.harlequinplus.com/freetrial.